THE SCIENCE (UN)FAIR

MIDDLE SCHOOL MAYHEM 3

C.T. WALSH

FARCICAL PRESS

COVER CREDITS

Cover design by Books Covered
Cover photographs © Shutterstock
Cover illustrations by Maeve Norton

Publisher's Cataloging-in-Publication Data

provided by Five Rainbows Cataloging Services

Names: Walsh, C.T., author.

Title: The science (un)fair / C.T. Walsh.

Description: Bohemia, NY : Farcical Press, 2019. | Series: Middle school mayhem, bk 3. | Summary: A wager and a cheating scandal test Austin's relationship with his girlfriend. | Audience: Grades 5 & up. | Also available in ebook and audiobook formats.

Identifiers: ISBN 978-1-950826-02-5 (paperback)

Subjects: LCSH: Bildungsromans. | CYAC: Middle school students--Fiction. | Middle schools--Fiction. | Cheating--Fiction. | Science fairs--Fiction. | Bullying--Fiction. | Humorous stories. | BISAC: JUVENILE FICTION / Social Themes / Adolescence & Coming of Age. | JUVENILE FICTION / School & Education. | JUVENILE FICTION / Humorous Stories. | JUVENILE FICTION / Boys & Men.

Classification: LCC PZ7.1.W35 Sc 2019 (print) | LCC PZ7.1.W35 (ebook) | DDC [Fic]--dc23.

For my Family

Thank you for all of your support

News flash. A new research study shows what we all already knew. No, chocolate milk does not come from brown cows. And no, kids don't really have a dessert stomach and a regular meal stomach. I'm talking about how middle school stinks, well, worse than adolescent kids stink in middle school. I mean, geez, would it kill these kids to take a test sniff every once in a while? And while we're on the subject, body spray does not equal a shower.

Some kids might like middle school because they're popular and their parents don't care if they get C's as long as they play sports, but for me, middle school was, well, different. It was my first year and I already had three nemesises. Is that a word? Nemeses? Nemesi? Whatever you call them, I had three of them, gunning for me from day one. Literally. My older brother, Derek, was one of them. He and his dumb butt chin have taunted me since the day I was born. I had the misfortune of being born eleven months after my brother, which puts me and his two butts in the same grade.

As if that wasn't bad enough, the school's most popular

kid had it out for me AND had a crush on my girlfriend. Oh, and the principal hated my guts and blamed me for just about everything that went wrong in the school. Full disclosure, it was only my fault about ten percent of the time. And he started it. But Principal Buthaire just saw the worst in me. If only he knew I was the one who coined his nickname, "Prince Butt Hair."

The next chapter in my middle school saga at Cherry Avenue Middle School began innocently enough as I entered my science class on a Monday afternoon. I was early as usual, which meant only a handful of students were there. Typically, I ended up chatting with my teacher, Mr. Gifford. I loved science and he was a pretty fun guy, although he didn't always have the best handle on his personal life.

I strolled into the lab and plopped my books onto the lab table as Mr. Gifford walked over to me with a smile.

"Nice turtleneck, sir. Goes great with the sports coat," I said with a thumbs up. I wasn't much of a fashion guru, but the college professor look wasn't exactly cutting edge.

"Thanks. What do you think of the beard?" He asked. I had recommended he grow a beard a few months back.

"Looking good," I said. I was afraid to ask if he had gotten any dates. He answered my question without me asking it.

"I have a new lady friend. Two months so far," he said, pleased with himself.

"That's great. I knew the beard would work."

"Yeah, she really likes it. I met her online. Filled out a bunch of questions and so did she and it said we're a perfect match!" He thought for a moment and then continued, "Although it's not always perfect. She doesn't like science. Any advice?"

I shrugged. "I'm eleven."

"Yeah, but you and Sophie are what I aspire to be with Audrey." Sophie was my girlfriend of a few months.

This was all getting way too complicated for me. "That's great. Maybe do a science lab with her or something. Maybe she'll learn to love it."

"Like dissect a frog?" Mr. Gifford asked.

"Not sure that's a great idea."

He rubbed his beard. "Yeah, she likes reptiles, so cutting them up probably wouldn't work."

Mr. Gifford reached up onto a shelf and grabbed a container of fish food. "Don't tell anyone, but since you're my favorite student, I'm putting you in charge of feeding Boomer. He's not eating much. I think he's mad at me for spending so much time with Audrey. She doesn't really like him, either."

I wasn't going to question why somebody would actually dislike a fish or whether or not fish had emotions. He was the science whiz, so I just nodded. We walked over to the fish tank behind my lab table. Boomer was a pretty chill angel fish. I wasn't sure if it was white with black stripes or black with white stripes. I have the same problems with zebras.

Mr. Gifford handed me the fish food and said, "Just give him a pinch every day and a little extra on Fridays."

"Pinch his cheeks or his butt?" I asked, trying not to laugh.

Mr. Gifford cracked up. "Good one, Austin."

"Seriously, I will take good care of him."

We stared at Boomer zip around the tank as I dropped a pinch of food on top of the water.

"Isn't it so peaceful? Did you ever just want to be a fish?" Mr. Gifford asked.

"Not really." Things were getting weird fast.

Mr. Gifford didn't seem to hear me. "Just leave all your troubles behind and hit the open sea?"

"It's dangerous out there, sir. Didn't you see Nemo?"

"Yeah, but the E.A.C. is totally rad." He gave me the surfer's hang loose sign and smiled. The bell rang, interrupting us.

Mr. Gifford turned around and said, "Okay, everyone. Settle down and listen up. I hope everyone had a great weekend. This is the start of my favorite time of year. I have good news."

Jake Gillespie called out, "Class is canceled?" Everyone cheered.

"No, no," Mr. Gifford said.

"Principal Buthaire quit?" Jake asked. Everyone cheered louder.

"No. One month from today, we will have the 44th annual Cherry Avenue Middle School Science Fair!"

I yelled out, "Yes!" and cheered wildly. I was actually pretty stoked about it. I loved science and knew I could win the whole thing. I looked around to see that I was the only one who seemingly felt that way, or at least was willing to show it to his peers. Everyone stared at me, even Sophie. I could feel my face flush red faster than a turbo toilet.

Mr. Gifford broke through the awkwardness. "Well that's the spirit, Austin!" and then continued, "Here's how it works."

I put my head down and started taking notes, ignoring the chuckles from Randy and others.

Mr. Gifford laid out the rules. "You can work alone or with one other partner. You cannot spend more than $200. I recommend a timeline and explanation of your project on a poster board. And you must present your project to the judges in an oral presentation."

"I'm out!" Kevin McManus said to chuckles.

My nemesis, Randy asked, "What do we get if we win?" Like he was gonna win.

"Good question, Mr. Warblemacher. You get Gopher pride," he said. Like anybody cared about that.

The class erupted into boos.

Mr. Gifford tried to salvage the situation, "And a really, nice medal, made of plastic..." His voice trailed off. Mr. Gifford shrugged to more boos, knowing his answer stunk. "Sorry. Budget cuts. But," he held up his index finger. "You also get bragging rights."

Great. Let's allow the winners to taunt the losers. Sounds like gym class for nerds. I didn't need bragging rights. I just liked building stuff, so I was in no matter what.

As if the science fair excitement wasn't enough (actually, for most, it wasn't), another bombshell dropped just after the eighth period bell. I stood at my locker, stuffing my backpack with notebooks and textbooks. Just Charles (don't dare call him Charlie or Chuck) walked up and spun the dial on his lock.

"Dude, I can't believe you didn't tell any of us."

I had no idea what he was talking about. "Umm, about what?"

"The website."

"I don't know anything about any website," I said. I threw up my hands. "Honest." I was always getting blamed for stuff. Forgive me if I was a little defensive.

Justin Allen walked by and whispered, "Nice work, Austin. You really got Butt Hair."

I turned around, confused. I checked my pants, wondering if somehow my butt had actually grown hair and was out for everyone to see. Luckily, my jeans were still firmly attached to my waist and there was no sign of any butt hair.

Just Charles opened his locker and then stared at me. "You really don't know? You didn't hear anything about Principal Buthaire's website?"

My shoulders dropped. I wished it was my butt hair. I didn't need another confrontation with Principal Buthaire. "What's on the website?"

"It lists so many different things. But basically, just bashing Prince Butt Hair at every turn, many of your battles."

"Really?" This was not good. Like, not at all.

"Dude, everyone thinks you did it."

Ahhhh, farts. "What? Oh, man. If everyone thinks I did it, then Butt Hair thinks I did it. He's gonna be on me like a smug look on Randy Warblemacher's face." Which was basically permanently.

"Dang, bro. Here he comes." Just Charles pointed down the hallway behind me.

I turned around to see Principal Buthaire heading down the hall, a man on a mission, checking everyone's faces in the small clusters of kids. In middle school, kids walk around like pack animals to avoid being easy prey for the mean kids. Herding is a survival mechanism. Whether you're a zebra or a tween, it works. Well, it works when your herd doesn't leave you in the dust.

I turned back to Just Charles, my herd, for some support, but he was gone. Double farts. That's why he wasn't my best friend. Ben would still be there. He'd be frozen stiff, but still, I'd feel better knowing he was behind me, thinking positive thoughts or whatever went on inside his head when he was frozen.

I slammed my locker quickly, knowing full well that I didn't have all my books. With my grades, I could afford to miss a homework or two. I slipped my backpack onto my shoulder and turned away from Principal Buthaire. I started to run, but was jerked backward. At first, I thought that Butt Hair had somehow caught up to me and grabbed onto my backpack with Hulk-like strength or maybe even lassoed me with his braided butt hair. I turned quickly and saw Principal Buthaire continuing to make his way toward me and that my shoulder strap was caught in the locker.

Principal Buthaire's voice echoed throughout the hallway. "Mr. Benson, you're late."

"But sir, school's over," Thomas Benson said in a high-pitched voice. At least Principal Buthaire was consistent in his unfairness.

"Well, I'm sure you're late for something. Your mother is probably waiting for you. She is, isn't she?"

"Yes, sir," Thomas said, defeated.

Instead of opening my locker back up, I grappled with the strap, struggling to pull it from behind the door. I forced it loose with a grunt and stumbled, nearly falling over. I turned on my heels with Principal Buthaire only one herd of kids behind me. I raced around a few kids, who were also scattering at the approaching Principal of Darkness.

"Mr. Davenport!" I heard Principal Buthaire call out. "I need a word with you!"

We would be having no words. Not even one. Not until I figured out more about this website and why I was going to get blamed for it. I continued down the hall until I saw Randy heading my way, a pack of his brute squad at his side. I stopped dead in my tracks. No matter which way I went, I would have a run in with one of my nemeses (I think I got it right this time). I looked to my left and saw an open classroom door. I scooted in quickly, not sure if Prince Butt Hair saw me enter or not.

I found myself face to face with Amanda Gluskin. Like face to face. So close that she looked like a Cyclops. You know what I'm talking about. I felt her tuna breath on my face and then up my unprotected nose. It was less than exciting. I nearly hurled.

"Austin," she whispered. "I didn't know you were so into me."

I backed up, Amanda's one eye becoming two again. I didn't know what to say. She wasn't the kind of girl you wanted to make angry. Her emotional outbursts were legendary. She once wrestled Mr. Muscalini over a confiscated note and won, forcing him into submission through the Camel Clutch. She was no joke. And also not great at reading situations. I was not at all into her.

"I just got turned around. I'm sorry to run into you like that." I wanted to run away. Fast. But I heard Principal Buthaire talking outside the classroom, so I was stuck for a while.

"I thought you had a girlfriend."

"I do. How's, umm, your dating life going?" I regretted it

immediately. She didn't have a dating life. Nobody had the guts to date her. Or the wrestling technique.

"It's better than ever," she said, raising an eyebrow.

"Oh, really?" I asked, surprised. "How so?"

"You're here."

Amanda stepped forward, licking her lips like I was a giant cheeseburger deluxe from Burger Boys.

"Well, it's been great, but I gotta go." I'd rather get accosted by Principal Buthaire than lovingly ingested by Amanda Gluskin. I turned quickly and sprinted from the room.

"Text me!" Amanda yelled after me.

I turned left at the corner and made another quick right turn, likely out of sight and reach of Principal Buthaire. I avoided a skirmish, but the war was still going, and the next battle was probably coming soon.

I still had to make it to Derek's locker and get to the bus. On days when Derek and I didn't stay after, I had to help him with his backpack. I know, not fair. The doofus broke his foot during a basketball game. We actually bonded over it a little because it was all Randy's fault. I know, what else is new? Randy Warblemacher: destroyer of all that is decent.

Well, that might be a stretch to say my brother was decent, but at that particular moment in time, Randy was my biggest foe, so the enemy of my enemy was my friend. Sort of.

Derek leaned forward on his crutches, his casted foot in the air behind him. "What took you so long?" he asked, annoyed.

There was no way I was going to mention Amanda Gluskin. I would never live that one down. And who knows what lengths my brother would go trying to set us up and ruin my life?

"I had to implement evasive maneuvers. Buthaire was on my trail. Sorry, Derek."

"You can call me Mr. Davenport," he said like an idiot. Nothing new there.

"I'm not your butler," I said, annoyed. "Besides, there are a lot of other things I'd rather call you than that."

Derek picked up and threw his backpack a few feet in front of me. "Let's go."

I shook my head. Derek swung through the hallway on his crutches. I took a few steps like a field goal kicker, took aim at the back of Derek's head, and surged forward.

"Davenport for the game winner!"

My foot connected with Derek's bag and almost shattered. "Owww!" I yelled. Apparently, kicking a bag full of textbooks was slightly different than a piece of leather filled with air. My bad.

Derek turned around to see me hopping around, holding my ankle, and spewing only the manliest of phrases like, "I want my mommy," and "My pinkie toe. My sweet, baby pinky toe is lost forever. I'll never be loved again..." You know, cool stuff that trends on Twitter and Instagram.

2

I approached the next day at school like I was in the witness protection program. Not only was Principal Buthaire after me about the website I found out absolutely nothing about, but Amanda Gluskin either wanted to date me or eat me, or both. And I didn't want clarification.

After getting off the bus, I pulled my hoodie up over my head and stared down at the ground, following Ben and Sammie from a safe distance. We navigated the chatty atrium without trouble. I had to split off from Ben and Sammie, heading to our lockers before Advisory. I kept my head down, using all of my other senses to guide me. But my senses failed me. I found myself staring at the overpriced and oversized shoes of one Randy Warblemacher. I looked up to see his smug smile.

"Good morning, Davenfart. I was thinking about you this morning."

"I try to avoid thinking about you."

Randy ignored me. "I know you fancy yourself a science whiz, although I did crush you in the balloon race. Do you remember that?"

I tried to forget it, but I often woke up in cold sweats with nothing but that on my mind. "What's your point?"

"Well, the idea of winning a plastic medal doesn't do much for me-"

"And you don't need any additional pride," I added, remembering Mr. Gifford's 'Gopher pride' comment.

He frowned at me and continued without responding to my comment, "So why don't we make this interesting? I mean, if you think you can win," he chortled.

"Oh, I most certainly do. What do you want to bet?"

"I want Sophie," he said.

"I can't give you Sophie in a bet, you idiot!"

He quickly countered, "Okay, your PlayStation then."

"That's reasonable." I thought about it for a moment. It was Derek's anyway. "And if I win, I want you to never speak to Sophie again."

"Not happening."

"Do you have Nintendo Switch?"

"Nah, maybe for my birthday."

"Okay, you can't talk to Sophie for the rest of middle school," I said.

"Nope. Rest of the year and you have a deal, if you win, of course. So, this won't ever happen."

"Don't bet on it," I said.

"I think we just did, Davenfart."

"Oh, yeah. You're right. For once."

I was ready for battle. Just not the one I was about to walk into. I turned on my heels and found myself staring into the severely unfashionable fish tie of Principal Buthaire, aka Prince Butt Hair. Who thought it would be a good idea to put fish on a tie? I mean, maybe as a joke, but I think he actually thought it looked good.

"Well, well, well. Mr. Davenport. Late again?"

I checked my watch. "Not yet." I tried to step around him. He slid his normally uncoordinated self in front of me smoothly.

"Oh, when we're done, you will be."

My shoulders slumped. Here we go again. It must be National Pick on Austin Day, which apparently was every Monday through Friday.

"We need to have a little chat."

Do we really?

Principal Buthaire peered down his nose at me. "Ever since you broke into my office, I've known you had advanced computer skills-"

"I did not..." I did, but he was never able to prove it.

He continued without acknowledging my rebuttal. "But what I didn't know was that you had website design skills, too." Principal Buthaire raised an eyebrow. "It seems as if you know what I'm talking about. You've got the look of the guilty."

"No, sir. Someone just told me about it. I had nothing to do with it. Is that all?"

"Not by a long shot. I know you did it. I'm going to prove it. And then I'm going to expel you like a painful little kidney stone."

I wasn't entirely sure how kidney stones were expelled from the body, but I imagined it couldn't be good. Regardless, I didn't want to get expelled. My parents would likely send me to military school. I wouldn't last one day. I can't imagine they have Epsom salt baths, after-school snacks, and certainly not Ben, Sophie, and Sammie.

"Can I go now, sir?"

Principal Buthaire smiled. "Not before you get your detention slip," he said it like it was ice cream.

"Sir, perhaps you want to laminate one for me so we don't kill so many trees? Or maybe go digital?"

"Don't annoy me, Mr. Davenport."

"Sorry." Not sorry. I took the detention slip and stepped around my nemesis of the moment.

"Remember, Mr. Davenport. I'm watching you. Kidney stone. Expelled."

3

I finally made it to class, walking into stares. Mr. White stopped his lecture and looked at me curiously.

"Do you have a late pass, Austin?"

"No, Principal Buthaire seems to think it's okay to stop me from getting to class and then give me detention for being late." I flashed my detention slip. "I'm sick of this place." I was still almost ready to bust out my prison costume that I wore when Prince Butt Hair first became Principal. It started a whole firestorm. I actually gave a presentation in front of the school board after he cancelled the Halloween dance.

I was still mad at last year's graduating eighth graders, who taped our former principal to the wall with duct tape for charity. They liked it so much they kept doing it until the school descended into chaos and the principal was fired and replaced with Principal Buthaire.

Anyway, back to class. Mr. White nodded and said, "Okay. We'll discuss it after class."

I gave him a big thumbs up and a sarcastic, "Can't wait," which was admittedly unnecessary and misdirected. I slumped into my desk, frustrated with my latest run in with Principal Buthaire.

I couldn't settle down. I was fidgeting and moving around, huffing and puffing. I didn't have to go to the bathroom, but I decided to go anyway. I needed a break.

We didn't have to ask permission to use the bathroom in math class, unlike other classes where you had to jump through every hoop imaginable short of bringing back a sample to prove to the teacher you actually went. That was the one rule we didn't have. Yet.

I strolled down the east wing. I could at least chill out at Max's. If you don't know who Max Mulvihill is, well, I'm not really sure, either. He's just this dude who runs his own private bathroom in the east wing of our school. I don't know how he does it or who he pays off, but he runs one of the best bathrooms around. And I've been in some pretty nice ones in the city. The kind that have cologne and mints. I'm a big fan of bathroom attendants, but my dad hates them. They do everything but wipe your butt for you. And in some really expensive places, they might even do that. But Dad is always complaining about having to pay to pee.

Anyway, Max and I had an agreement. I helped him with his business, giving him various marketing and organizational tips, and he lets me pee (not poop) for free. I know, he drives a hard bargain, but it was better than nothing.

I pushed open the door slowly and slipped into Max's Comfort Station, as he recently rebranded. Max was waiting as usual.

"Aus the Boss, what's up, dude?" He said in his manly voice. I had no idea how old Max was, but I once made the mistake of asking him if he had kids. He's probably twenty or thirty or something.

"Hey, Max." I gave him a high five and looked around the room.

Nearly every time I went in the bathroom, the decor was different. I've seen table games from foosball to ping pong, Ms. Pacman, some sort of heavy-metal pinball machine, and even the Down the Clown target game. He's had a massage chair that I'm pretty certain he stole from the mall, a hammock, and a Lazy Boy recliner. During state testing, he has essential oils (I love the lavender), and brain foods like blueberries, avocados, and broccoli. (Nobody eats the broccoli).

I wiped my brow. It was a little hot in there, and then I noticed that part of the room was sectioned off. Steam rose from above a wood-paneled privacy screen. I heard a hum and bubbles gurgling from behind it.

"That's extra, dude," Max said.

"What is it?" I peeked my head around to see a four-person hot tub surrounded by tiki torches.

"That's the spa," he said as if it was totally normal to have a hot tub in a middle school bathroom.

"Dude! How do you get away with this?" I asked.

"Trade secret, bro."

"Do people actually use it?"

"No doubt." Max walked up next to me. "A lot of kids come here instead of lunch or fake illness and pretend to go to the nurse. I have to limit usage so nobody gets caught skipping days of school at a time. I learned that one the hard way. Devan Chung's whole body turned into a giant prune after cutting a day of classes."

"Makes sense." I looked around and scratched my head. "How did you even get it in here?"

"Mirrors," he said, simply.

That made sense. Max Mulvihill, the Magician. The dude was the Harry Potter of middle school bathrooms.

Max interrupted my thoughts. "Do you have any business you need to attend to at this time?"

"Huh, what? Oh, no." I shook my head. "I don't have to go. I just need to chill for a few minutes."

"Tough day?"

"How'd you know?"

"It's my job to know."

"It is?"

"This is a full-service establishment. You know that," Max said, like I had a brain fart.

"This new website bashing Buthaire is driving me nuts."

"There was a new posting today."

"Really?"

"So, it's not you behind it?"

"I swear. I don't know why I'm always getting in trouble from Butt Hair. The dude has it in for me." I always seemed to use the word 'dude' more when I was with Max. Because I assure you, Principal Buthaire was no dude. "Please spread the word. I want to find out who did it. What does the latest post say?"

Max turned and walked over to a free-standing cabinet

and opened it. He looked back at me over his shoulder and said, "I normally charge extra for this, so consider this a one-time thing." He pulled out an iPad, turned to me, and typed in a password.

"This is the Disney of bathrooms," I said in amazement.

"Funny you should mention that. I was just studying Disney. I might let you poop for free here if you could come up with some good mascot ideas. Do you think kids would come here more if we had a mascot in a suit?"

I furrowed my brow. "Not sure that would be a big draw."

Max looked disappointed.

I quickly continued, "Would it sign autographs and take pictures?"

"Maybe?" he shrugged. "I'm still strategizing."

"I'll think about. It could work." I wasn't certain of it, but I didn't want to get on Max's bad side. His services were very convenient.

Max smiled and then returned to the iPad. He pressed the Safari app. After a few more key strokes, he held it out to me. I looked down to see the anti-Buthaire website with a fresh post, outlining Principal Buthaire chasing me down the hallway yesterday!

I couldn't believe it. But even more than that, Max surprised me again. "You have Wi-Fi?"

"Of course. What kind of a bathroom do you think this is?"

"I was thinking like a real bathroom."

"Does a real bathroom have a sushi bar?"

"You have a sushi bar?"

"No, that would be ridiculous. I was just messing with you," Max laughed.

I looked at the website as Max scrolled. It had a picture of the Prince of Butt Hair yelling at a student, spit flying from his mouth. It was really appetizing. It then went on to list a running detention counter, which appeared to be increasing faster than the national debt, and a variety of ridiculous policies implemented since the beginning of the year.

I shook my head. "I don't know what I'm going to do about this."

"You gotta get to the bottom of this," Max said. "I'll keep an ear out. And get me some mascot ideas."

"Absolutely. Thanks for the hospitality, as always."

AFTER THE BELL RANG, I rushed from math class. I wanted to catch up with Sophie before our next class to ask her to be my science fair partner. I hustled down the hall and saw her up ahead of a small pack. I ran to catch up to her. Mr. Muscalini, my gym teacher, might not call it running, but it was my version, anyway. I stopped next to her, catching my breath. In that moment, I realized I needed to play fewer video games or at least find video games that required physical movement without dancing.

"Hey," I said.

Sophie smiled. "Hey. I've barely seen you today."

"Principal Buthaire made me late again, so I missed you on the way to math," I said, through heavy breathing.

Sophie rolled her eyes. "Oh, my God. He's unbelievable."

"We rushed out of science yesterday, so I never got to ask you. Do you want to be my partner-" I took a deep breath in. Sophie looked at me like I was about to propose or something. I continued, "In the science fair?"

Sophie's face dropped. "Oh, no. I thought you would ask Ben. I can't. I already have a partner."

I could feel my stomach begin to reject the seafood surprise I ate in the cafeteria, which note to self, it should've been doing already. I needed to go to the doctor to figure out why my stomach wasn't working properly.

"Who, who, who-" I stuttered, "is your partner?" I asked, fearing that it would be none other than Randolph Warblemacher, my evil nemesis.

"Randy," she said quietly, perhaps hoping I wouldn't hear.

"Here we go again," I muttered, even lower than Sophie spoke.

"What did you say?" Sophie asked. I couldn't tell if she was annoyed or really not sure what I said.

I couldn't hold back the anger that was rapidly building. "This is Santukkah! all over again." Randy tried to steal Sophie from me during the school musical.

"What do you mean?" Sophie asked, this time definitely annoyed.

"Randy trying to steal you from me."

"Do you own me?" She stared at me with her hands on her hips.

I huffed. "You know what I mean. If it's not reading lines, it's doing homework or science projects. Why does he always ask you?"

Sophie put her hand on my shoulder. "It was an honest mistake."

I controlled my anger a touch. "Okay, so tell him you made a mistake and that we are going to be partners."

"I can't. I already made a commitment. He told me a bunch of his ideas. I can't leave now."

Grrrr.

And to make matters worse, after that, I had gym class with Randy. It was always bad, but after the science fair snafu, it was particularly terrible. And Mr. Muscalini made it worse.

The entire class stood across the baseline of the basketball court after attendance. Mr. Muscalini faced us and stepped forward wearing shorts that were way too short. I stared at them.

"Davenport, what's the problem?"

I didn't know what to say. "I, umm, like your shorts, sir." A couple of kids chuckled.

"You know what I always say-"

"Don't stop running unless your brain is hemorrhaging?" I asked.

"Yes, that's true, but I was thinking more of 'when the sky is out, take those thighs out!' or is it, 'when the sun's aloft, show those thighs off!'"

"But, we're inside the gym, sir."

Mr. Muscalini shook his head. "Never mind. Let's move on. I'm very excited to tell you that it's rope week!"

Everybody groaned, even the athletic kids.

Mr. Muscalini continued, pacing the gym, "We're gonna do Tug o' War, rope climbing, jump roping, the Tarzan swing. You're gonna love it."

It sounded like a nerd's worst nightmare, but there was no avoiding it at that point.

"Okay! Let's go. Everybody over to the rope!"

Mr. Muscalini pointed to a fifty-foot rope hanging from the rafters of the gym ceiling. He led us over to it and lined us up. I slipped into the crowd, walking as slowly as I could, hoping other students would pass me. Most times, a nerd's best chance at success in gym was the bell ringing before getting a turn.

Unfortunately, Mr. Muscalini had a different idea. "Davenport, why don't you lead us off, as a thank you for the wardrobe comment? Even tough guys like me need help sometimes to feel good inside."

"That's okay, sir. I don't want to cut anyone on line." I said, peeking out behind Ben, and then disappearing again.

"Davenport, report for duty. Now, soldier!"

My shoulders slumped. I didn't want to go first. I was going to embarrass myself. At least everyone else would feel good about beating me. I walked up to Mr. Muscalini and stopped in front of the mat underneath the rope.

I heard Randy say, "Hey, Davenfart, what are those strings hanging out from your shorts? Oh, wait. Those are your legs." Randy's idiot friends chuckled.

I looked at Mr. Muscalini and then up at the rope, which seemed to disappear into the clouds above. "Sir, isn't this dangerous? It's like forty or fifty feet up, no safety harness, and this two-inch-thick mat that's only two feet wide?" I made the best case I could to stop this disaster before it started.

Mr. Muscalini looked down at me and yelled, "Life doesn't have safety harnesses, Davenport!"

"Sir, why are you screaming? I'm right here."

He lowered his voice to a whisper, "Sorry, life doesn't have safety harnesses, Davenport."

"Yeah, but I don't see why any of us should have to risk serious injuries."

Mr. Muscalini waved me off. "It's okay, we have insurance. A lot of it. Once, Mrs. Felix left a grade school kid on the bus for like six hours. We got sued out the yin yang and the school didn't even have to pay a cent."

"That's really soothing. Thank you for that."

"Quit stalling, Davenport. It's time to shine. Who's the man?"

"Uh, me?"

"Like you mean it, Davenport!"

Really? How embarrassing could you get? I sucked it up and yelled, "I'm the man!"

"You ready to unleash the beast? Do it now!"

It actually worked. Unleash the beast! Energy surged through my body. I could do it!

"Who's got this?" Mr. Muscalini yelled.

"I got this!" I yelled. Most kids laughed. I didn't care. I was ready.

"That's the spirit, Davenport!"

I stepped up to the rope and exhaled with force. I shook out my arms and legs and stretched my neck from side to side. I finished off my warm up by cracking my knuckles.

I jumped with such force, I felt the air surge through my hair. Like a rocket ship breaking through the atmosphere. I grabbed hold of the rope with both hands and squeezed it between my feet. I reached up and pulled. Again. And again. And again. With each pull, I let out a warrior-like battle cry.

I was crushing it. I didn't want to look down. I was afraid I might get scared. But I looked over at the other students when I heard them laughing. I was expecting them to be tiny little specs of people like houses look when you see them out of an airplane window. The funny thing was, at least to everyone but me, was that they were full size right next to me. I looked down to see myself swinging on the rope only a foot off the ground.

I actually had to look up at some of them, including Randy, who said, "Unleash the beast. Not the geek."

I hopped off and slunked back to the end of the line. Mr. Muscalini was apparently speechless for the first time since I met him.

A slew of kids followed. Some good. Some bad. Ben swung around in a nice circle. It was nearly perfect. He told me he was just trying to make me feel better, but I knew he was just making excuses.

Randy stepped up to the rope. I didn't want to watch. I figured he would be able to do it with his teeth or upside down or something. Perhaps he would just walk up the rope without even needing to hold onto anything. He could wave to the cheerleaders and sign autographs and stuff.

I wasn't that far off. He jumped up and climbed the rope like a monkey. He didn't even use his feet. He just reached up and pulled himself higher with his arms. In less than a minute, he had touched the ceiling, rang the bell, and slid back down to the ground to cheers.

Mr. Muscalini looked at his stopwatch. "Warblemacher, that was the fastest time I've seen since, well, ever. I can't even do it that fast."

That's what I was up against, kids.

4

Later that night, I sat alone in our living room, reclined on the couch with a blank paper in front of me. Science was on my mind. Well, not really. The only thing that came to mind when trying to figure out a winning science idea was a black hole. And that was when I wasn't thinking about Randy trying to charm Sophie while doing their project. So that night wasn't much better than the day.

Derek's foot pain was also so unbearable; apparently, he was only capable of breathing. I'm surprised he didn't ask me to do that for him, too. I drew a picture of me stomping on Derek's foot while I brainstormed. I was interrupted by a text from, you guessed it, Derek the Dying.

It read, "Need chocolate milk. Shaken not stirred. Chilled glass. Not plastic."

"You've got to be kidding me," I whined as I stood up.

I walked out of the room and into the kitchen. My mom was straightening up. I pulled the fridge door open, the jars and bottles shaking on the shelf.

My mom looked over at me with a frown. "Everything okay?"

"No. I'm tired of being Derek's errand boy. He acts like he's running out of time."

She chuckled. "I know he's hamming it up a little. The cast will be off soon."

"Can we cast up his face?" Or his texting thumbs, at least?

"Honey, be nice."

"He just asked to have his chocolate milk in a chilled glass, shaken not stirred. Is he the long-lost son of James Bond or something?" It might explain why he and I were so different.

My mom laughed. "No. Just get him the chocolate milk in a regular glass."

I grabbed the milk and chocolate syrup and closed the fridge.

My mother asked, "Everything else okay?"

"Yes," I lied. I didn't feel like talking about it.

I was thankful to hear the doorbell ring. "Can you bring this to Derek? I'll get the door."

"Sure," my mom said.

I handed my mother the glass, then hustled through the hallway and pulled open the door to see my best friend, Ben.

"Come on in," I said, holding the door for him.

Ben followed me to my room as we chatted. I closed the door behind us. I hopped on my bed while Ben plopped into the bean bag chair.

"Oh, that's nice," he said, relaxing.

"What's up?"

"I didn't get a chance to talk to you after school. My mom picked me up early for the dentist."

"Sorry to hear that."

"Me, too. Why does the dentist ask me so many questions about my life with his hands in my mouth?"

"I don't know. So, what's up?"

"Oh, I wanted to make sure we were going to enter the science fair together."

"Of course," I said. I wasn't going to tell him that I asked Sophie first.

"What's the matter?"

"Nothing," I said. "Something. Everything."

"Sophie trouble?"

"How'd you know?"

"Well, I've analyzed your relationships. You have four major stressors: Principal Buthaire, Randy, and your brother, Derek, all of whom make you more angry than anything. Sophie is the only one who makes you sad."

I shrugged. He was right. Ben's mother was a psychologist.

"What happened?" Ben asked.

"She partnered with Randy for the science fair." I almost vomited after I said it.

"Oooh, low blow," Ben said. "So, let's crush them."

"I just want to crush him," I said. "I'm not happy with Sophie, but she's still my girlfriend."

"What kind of project are you thinking about?" Ben asked.

"I've got lots of potential ideas," I lied. "Swirling around in my head, just waiting to come out."

"You don't have anything, do you?"

"Nope. Nothing," I said. Grrr was rapidly becoming my catch phrase.

~

I KNEW I wanted to crush Randy, but I had zero idea how to do it. I researched like crazy, but couldn't come up with an idea. The best I could come up with was the completely uncreative and boring erupting volcano, which should be banned from all future science fairs. It's something my brother would do. Either that or partner with a smart girl who's not smart enough to not have a crush on him, who would end up doing the entire project for him. So, he'd get a solid B while doing no work. He's got the butt chin, so my parents would probably be good with that. Me? That would never happen. Plus, Sophie is the only girl who has a crush on me (Amanda Gluskin, you ask? No. Just no.) Sometimes, I wonder what the heck a girl like Sophie is doing with a nerd like me.

Back to the science fair. Randy and Sophie would be a difficult duo to beat. Randy was smart, competitive, and devious. Sophie was smart, a hard worker, and a very good presenter. Not to mention, I could win the science fair and lose my girlfriend, so I had to keep Randy from asking Sophie out and keep my worrying from spinning out of control, which wasn't a strength of mine. I always viewed having Sophie as a girlfriend as being too good to be true.

Ben headed home, so I was back in the living room, note pad on my lap. At that point, I had two ideas. First was a fart-suppression device, which I thought would have huge real-life applications and explosive sales potential, but I wasn't sure how to keep people from actually exploding if they didn't get their farts out. It was kind of a problem. True, I could get the same insurance that the school had, but I believed it was morally wrong to create a device that caused people to explode if they ate too much spicy food. Call me crazy.

The second idea was a human catapult. I just thought it

would be cool to catapult to school instead of take the dumb bus. I'm sure Zorch would let us put a giant, blow-up landing pad on the roof. He was our custodian and a trusted confidant.

"I'm hungry," Derek whined from the den next door.

I put my head back and closed my eyes. "This is unbelievable," I whispered to myself.

"Ask somebody else," I yelled out.

"Dad's still at work and mom went to pick up Leighton," Derek said, throwing out a few coughs out at the end. I wasn't falling for it. "Come on, dude. I'm going to the basketball game when Mom gets back. I need to eat before then. I need energy to support my teammates."

"You're an athletic supporter?"

"I guess so," he said, seemingly not sure why I was asking. I guess he didn't know that his jock strap was also called an athletic supporter.

I wanted to try something. In gym, I realized that if you yell stuff with authority, people tended to answer questions more readily. So, I did my best Mr. Muscalini impression, "Say it with pride!"

Derek yelled, "I'm an athletic supporter!"

I laughed to myself. Sometimes my brother's not so bad or at least not so smart that I can't have a little fun with him.

"Can I get my food now?" Derek asked.

"In ten minutes. I'm finishing something up," I called out

"I'm hungry now. I want an omelet or French toast," Derek said.

"I'm not a chef. You get whatever I can pick up and bring you."

Not that I was in much of a creative state of mind to begin with, but Derek certainly ended my brainstorming session. I stood up in a huff and headed over to the kitchen.

"Please, just cook me some eggs. It's simple. Over easy. With cheese on top of that. Oh, and bacon. Side of toast to soak up the yolks. And butter on the side of that," Derek said.

"This isn't a diner. The only egg you're going to get is one cracked over your head."

Leighton walked in and said, "I would pay to see that. In fact, I might join you in doing it. We have at least two dozen eggs in the fridge."

"I thought you said nobody was here?" I asked Derek.

Derek called out, "Oops." It was not believable. He was not nearly as good an actor as Randy was.

I looked over at Leighton for sympathy. "I wish I could buy a robot that could do all of his dirty work, like a butler."

"That'd be nice," she said, smiling.

And then it hit me. "Science fair!" I yelled.

"What?" Leighton asked, confused.

"I figured out my science fair project!" I rushed out of the kitchen and down the hall to my room. I was super pumped. I couldn't wait to tell Ben.

I heard Derek call out, "Hey, what about my eggs?"

"Sorry, sucka!" I yelled over my shoulder. If my plans were the least bit devious, I would've cackled and twirled my invisible, sinister mustache.

5

After my eureka moment, I spent the rest of the night sketching out some basic ideas for my robot butler. Making progress on crushing Randy energized me a little. But not a lot. I had a winning project idea, but I still had a girlfriend who had partnered with Randy and I knew he wouldn't stop until he had won her over.

I wasn't overly enthused when it was time for science the next day. Thankfully, we wouldn't be working on our science fair projects in class, so I would be able to work with Sophie instead of her working with Randy. Still, things were a bit tense since she promised to work with him.

I rounded the corner, heading toward science class when I saw Mrs. Lynch, the Communications teacher, talking to Principal Buthaire, who had his back to me next to the door. I hoped they weren't waiting to communicate my getting expelled like a kidney stone.

As I approached, I saw Mrs. Lynch look in my direction. I put my finger to my lips in a shushing signal. She looked back at Principal Buthaire as if I were invisible. Good. Not getting expelled. Yet.

I gave her a thumbs up as I slipped by. I heard Principal Buthaire say, "We need to build a marketing campaign so the kids feel good about school again."

I stood inside the classroom door, continuing to listen.

Mrs. Lynch asked, "Why not just change some of the rules that make them feel bad about school?"

"No, I like those." He laughed like she was an idiot. "We just need the students to feel good in spite of those rules that make them feel bad."

"I'm confused," Mrs. Lynch said.

"Don't worry about the rules. Let's just put together some things that make me look good."

"Riiiight," Mrs. Lynch said. I got the feeling she had no idea how to do that.

"Good," Principal Buthaire said. "Sounds like we're on the same page. Hurry off to class. I'd hate to give you a detention for being late."

Mrs. Lynch chuckled nervously. I wasn't sure if Prince Butt Hair was serious or not.

Billy Madison walked into class and frowned at me, as I stood against the wall like a weirdo.

"Making out with the wall again, Davenfart?"

"You can never practice too much," I said, and walked as cool as I could over to my lab table. Mr. Gifford met me on my way.

"Austin, my boy, I've been dying to know what your project is going to be. You'll be working with Sophie, I presume?"

"Umm, no. Ben, actually."

"Oh. Will Sophie be participating?" Mr. Gifford asked.

"Yes," I said, not willing to offer any additional information.

"Who will she partner with?"

"Umm, not sure. I'm working with Ben Gordon." I said it again to try to deflect any discussion of Sophie and Randy.

"Oooh, that's a good combo. I like our, err, your chances."

I had heard that Mr. Gifford and the other science teachers all bet on whose students would win. His slip seemed to confirm that.

"So what's your project going to be?"

I shrugged sheepishly and smiled. "It's super-secret. All I can tell you is that I am really pumped about it. It's going to be awesome."

"Awww, I hate secrets," Mr. Gifford whined. "Please? Pretty please with cherries on top?"

"Sorry. Can't be too careful," I said, shaking my head. Sometimes, I felt like I was the adult when I was with Mr. Gifford. Or that we were two kids.

"But perhaps I could be of some assistance?" Mr. Gifford raised an eyebrow. "There's nothing in the rules against a little guidance. This will be my 32nd science fair since I've started working here at Cherry Avenue. That's a wealth of experience that could help me crush Ms. Epstein, er help you win."

I was intrigued. While I was reasonably confident that I could beat Randy, a little insurance help could be useful. I tapped my pursed lips, thinking. I did have a lot of work ahead of me. Not just building, but a lot of designing and complex electronical (is that a word?) work that needed to be done. I wouldn't ask him to do any of it, but he was smart and could help me win or at least beat Randy. Having the teacher on your side can be very beneficial.

"Okay, you're speaking my language." I said, "But you can't tell anyone. Pinky promise?"

"Done." We locked pinkies. "My lips are sealed," Mr. Gifford said.

I leaned in and told Mr. Gifford my secret project.

THE NEXT FEW days went by quickly. Ben and I had been holed up in my room, which had transformed (I love Transformers, by the way, but no pun intended) into robot-building headquarters. We were still in research and design mode, so my room was filled with books, crumpled up sketches, empty juice boxes, and cheese stick wrappers. You know, the essentials.

On Tuesday morning, I actually woke up by rolling over onto a half-drunk Capri-Sun that squirted me in the eye. Hey, at least it was better than when Derek dunked my wrist in a bowl of warm water and I woke up wishing I had worn a diaper like the time I slept outside Sophie's house. But that's a story for another day.

Still on a modest sugar-high from drinking what was left of the Capri-Sun (post eye squirt), Ben, Sammie, and I walked off the bus and into the atrium. There were more students than normal who were milling about and talking.

I looked around curiously and then froze like Ben usually did in a pressure situation. Principal Buthaire was in the corner to my left, a group of kids surrounding him. He was also under the tree and next to the water fountain to my right. I spun around, disoriented.

"What...is...happening?" I said, my pulse skyrocketing. "My worst fear has manifested itself!" I dropped to my knees. "My nemesis has cracked the code to the universe. He controls time! I will be late forever and have eternal detention!"

"Oh, my God," Ben whispered and then laughed. He looked at me and said, "You alright?"

"He's...everywhere. How is this possible?" My mouth remained open in shock.

Ben and Sammie laughed. Sammie said, "They're cardboard cutouts, dummy."

The blood returned to my face and brain. I looked at all of the Butt Hairs and realized Sammie was right. I exhaled and wiped the sweat off my brow. I stood up and dusted off my jeans.

"What the heck is he doing with all those?" Ben asked.

And then Mrs. Lynch hit me. Well, she didn't actually hit me, but I remembered her conversation that I overheard with Principal Buthaire. "It's part of his marketing campaign to win the students back," I said, as we walked over to one of the cutouts. "I forgot to tell you I overheard him talking to Mrs. Lynch."

"Win the students back?" Ben questioned. "You say that like any of us ever liked him."

Sammie and I laughed. We got a close-up look at a life-size cardboard cutout of Principal Buthaire giving a thumbs up. A word bubble exclaimed, "Who's cooler than this guy?"

"How many people are there in the world?" I asked.

"Like seven billion," Ben said.

"So, I'm guessing like all of those people are cooler than he is," I said. "Except Randy."

Ben laughed. Sammie pursed her lips and stared me down. She was Team Randy. It was hurtful.

I shook my head, but said nothing. People's love of Randy was one of the few things that could shut me up.

"Was that the bell?" Ben asked, attempting to change the subject.

"We better hustle," I said, a hop in my step.

"I didn't hear anything," Sammie said, frowning.

"I definitely heard it. Let's go!" I said, speeding up to a run.

NOTHING MUCH HAPPENED until science class. Sophie and I sat at our lab table analyzing fossil patterns in rock strata. It was riveting stuff. Sophie looked over at me as I studied a slide under a microscope.

"How funny are Principal Buthaire's cardboard cutouts?" she asked.

"I thought they were real and that he was everywhere. I almost pooped myself."

Sophie laughed. "What are you doing for your science project?"

I stood up and looked at her. "Sorry. It's a secret."

"You're not gonna tell me?" Sophie asked, annoyed.

"I'm sorry. I don't want Randy to know."

"We're not going to cheat."

"I trust you. I will never trust him. He cheated in the crying contest."

"Really, Austin?"

"I can't win," I muttered to myself. I looked at Sophie and said, "Okay. You want to know what my project is going to be? I'll tell you. It's a Randy Remover."

"Real mature, Austin. Sometimes, you're a real jerk."

"Yep. It's all my fault," I said.

6

I threw myself into the science project. Ben and I had designed a sweet mobile robot that could pick up things for its master using voice commands. The plans were great. The only problem was we had to actually build it and make it work. You could design the best teleportation device, but that doesn't mean your butt particles are going anywhere.

We were even meeting before school. That's how badly I wanted to beat Randy in the contest. Ben and I sat in our usual bean bag chairs, which were my favorites. Their decorational and furnitural versatility was unmatched, although a good futon was a clear second.

Staring at the ceiling, I asked Ben, "How do we keep it under $200?"

"I know. It's a problem. The technological marvel that is Handsy is quite expensive."

"Handsy?" I asked.

"Yeah, that's what I named him."

"That's a big decision to make without me," I said, surprised. "I don't like it."

"Oh, what about Grabriella?"

"No," I said, shaking my head. "What about Handsome? To activate it, you could say, 'Hey, Handsome!'"

"Not bad," Ben said, nodding his head and weighing the name. "I like it."

"Do you think we could program it to have an 'accidental' malfunction and slap Derek in the face? Repeatedly?" I asked, laughing.

"I think that should be phase two. We've got a lot of work ahead of us," Ben said.

"You're right. We need to keep it under $200. A slapping mechanism with enough power to knock Derek out sounds expensive. How do we keep the cost down?" I said, tapping my chin. "How about the county electronic recycling place?"

"That's a thing?' Ben asked, furrowing his brow.

"Yes. I bet they have old video cameras, lenses, microphones, maybe even some computer chips."

"That could work. We could buy a part or two on eBay if we need to," Ben added.

"What about the outside? I asked. "How are we going to hold it all together?"

"Right. We don't want it to look like a rolling junk yard, wires hanging out everywhere."

We could put it in a soda bottle or something," Ben said.

"I don't think that'll hold the weight."

"What about 3D parts? I bet we can get some time on the 3D printer at the library."

Ben said, "Yes. But we'd better block off some time, though. It's only available at certain times and we don't know if anyone else will want to use it for their project."

I popped up from my bean bag chair, well, as much as you can pop up from a giant, mushy vacation from life that functions as a seat. "It's starting to come together, Benjamin!"

Ben rolled out of his seat with enthusiasm and I readied myself for a windmill high five. I got into a solid stance and started winding my left arm as fast as I could. Ben did the same.

"Here it comes! You ready?" I yelled.

"Bring it!" Ben yelled.

I unleashed a ferocious five, thrusting my entire body forward. I pushed my hand forward with such force, it caused me to squeeze my eyes shut. My hand hit nothing but air. The force of my five carried me forward. My body crumpled onto my desk, knocking my light and a stack of comics and papers to the ground. I fell into one of the bean bag chairs with a 'ploof!' (That's a real word, I think.)

"You okay?" Ben asked, staring down at me with concern on his face.

My pride was a little hurt, but the rest of me felt fine. "Totally," I said, "Bean bags to the rescue!"

If you've never been around high-fiving nerds, be careful. There's no telling what could go wrong.

DESPITE THE HIGH-FIVING FAILURE, Ben and I were on a high. We had a great plan and a bunch of good ideas on how to implement it. And then somebody had to go and ruin it.

Walking into school, Ben, Sammie, and I saw kids gathered around all the cardboard cutouts again. This time, they were pointing and laughing. I thought they were pretty funny before. Well, after I realized they were fake.

"What's going on?" Sammie asked Ishan Meeka.

Ishan pointed at the cardboard cutouts of Principal

Buthaire and said, "Somebody defaced all of the Principal's pictures." He laughed. "They're pretty funny."

We walked over to the cutout that said, "Who's cooler than this guy?" Maggie Blatch, a tall volleyball player (is there any other kind?) stood in front of the cutout, but we could see in huge letters, graffiti that read, 'Everybody!'

Ben, Sammie, and I studied the handwriting. "Well, we kinda knew that already," I said.

There was more. As Maggie stepped out of the way, the artist drew what looked quite like the picture I drew on in the Butt Crack (Principal Buthaire's office). I had broken in to the Butt Crack around Halloween to right some wrongs and added a few wrongs myself, like drawing a mustache on his wife and changing his computer sounds so that every time he got an email, it would make a fart sound. I know. Real mature. I've grown up a lot in those few months. That was like forever ago.

Anyway, this picture had huge horns sprouting from Principal Buthaire's forehead, a big handlebar mustache, and a few blackened teeth. I wished I had thought of the teeth when I was in his office creating my own masterpiece.

"Off to class, now. Off to class," Dr. Dinkledorf's voice echoed behind me.

I turned as he approached.

"Austin. I trust you had nothing to do with this?"

"No, sir," I said, looking him in the eye. Dr. Dinkledorf had seen me take out some of Prince Butt Hair's prison/security cameras, and even encouraged me to stand up against the ridiculous rules, but I wasn't sure how he would feel about pure vandalism.

Zorch walked up behind Dr. Dinkledorf, a cardboard cut-out under his arm. "Admiring your handywork?" Zorch asked. "You look a little too proud."

"I didn't do it," I said, throwing my arms up in the air. "Why does everybody blame me first without question?"

Zorch looked me in the eye. "I'm sorry. I believe you."

"Me, too," Dr. Dinkledorf said.

"I hope so. I swear on Sophie and Star Wars that I didn't do it."

"Wow. I'm convinced." Ben pointed to the cutout under Zorch's arm. "What happened to that one?"

"Defaced, like all the others." Zorch held it out for us to see. It said, "Make it a great day!" Written next to it, the graffiti bandit had written, "No! You can't make me, Butt Hair!" And you guessed it, the picture had some additions on it, mainly, lots of butt hair flowing out of the Principal's pants.

We all chuckled a bit and then looked around to make sure Prince Butt Hair nor any of his minions were lurking.

"Too bad none of the cameras are working," Dr. Dinkledorf said with a wink. "Make it a great day!" Dr. Dinkledorf smiled and then shuffled off with his briefcase.

You may recall, Principal Buthaire had bamboozled the school board for funding to add security cameras. He used them for his own ruthless pleasure. After being alerted to the fact that Principal Buthaire was using the security cameras to give out detentions for being late and other minor infractions, the Superintendent and school board decided the security cameras would only turn on during lock downs, fire alarms, and other emergencies. It was a big win for freedom. Detentions plummeted to all-time lows. Well, at least since Principal Buthaire was in charge.

Zorch put the cutout under his arm again and said, "I got a few more pickups to do."

"Okay. I'm a little mad at you," I said.

"I'm sorry, buddy. You and he have too much history. You were a legitimate suspect."

It was true, but unfair to jump to conclusions. "If you figure out who did it, please let me know. I'm sure I'll be the first one Prince, er, Principal Butt, er, Buthaire blames."

"Will do," Zorch said with a salute. He headed off, a 2D version of Principal Buthaire under his arm. I wished he would take the 3D version away, too.

I SAT IN ADVISORY, talking to Just Charles after the morning announcements and before the bell rang for first period. "I almost wish we still had the cameras working."

"No, you don't," he said, laughing.

"Well, as much as I hated them, it would've saved me from this. I know I'll be blamed."

And sure enough, no sooner had I taken my next breath, I heard the Speaker of Doom crackle, perhaps signaling what would eventually result in my last breath. In case you don't know, the Speaker of Doom was like the opposite of the Bat Signal. Principal Buthaire used it to summon me when he wanted to accuse me of something that I most likely didn't do. I said most likely. Sometimes, I did do it, but it's just wrong to assume I ALWAYS do it.

Ms. Tilles, one of the secretaries in the main office, moaned through the speaker, seemingly bored of calling me down to the office, "Austin Davenport to see Principal Buthaire. Again."

I stood up to stares. I was pretty used to it by that point. I had become somewhat of a hero, standing up to The Man. I didn't sign autographs or have a star on Cherry Avenue or anything, but a lot of kids appreciated my civil disobedience.

I saluted my teacher, Mrs. Callahan, and said, "If I'm not

back tomorrow, I'll most likely be at LaSalle Military Academy for Delinquent Youth. It's been a pleasure, ma'am."

My class laughed, including Mrs. Callahan.

"You're the drama king," Just Charles said.

"I didn't choose this life, bro," I said, slinking out of the class.

I entered Prince Butt Hair's evil lair, which I previously dubbed The Butt Crack. Principal Buthaire looked up from the magazine he was reading. It was either 'Horrific Principal's Digest' or 'The Idiot's Idiotic Guide to Idiotically Being an Idiot'. I wanted to find out which one, but didn't have the courage to ask. Either way, I bet he had lifetime subscriptions to both.

"You wanted to see me, sir?" I asked instead.

"Sit down, Mr. Davenport," he said, firmly. We stared at each other for a moment. I wasn't sure if he was playing mind games with me or practicing for a staring contest. He also could've been stalling so he could make me late for my next class and give me detention. Finally, he began, "You must think you're really smart, don't you?"

I didn't know how to answer that. "I get straight As and am a member of the National Honors Society."

"What did you get in physical education last quarter, Mr. Davenport?" Principal Buthaire asked, as if he had just won the presidential debates.

"Umm, a B, sir."

"So we've established you are deceitful. A B does not mean straight As."

I shrugged. "Okay, you got me. I can't do pull-ups. I'm smart enough to know why I'm here, sir. And I didn't do it. You don't want to believe me, that's fine. You never do. But you have no proof. It would be impossible if you did."

Principal Buthaire chuckled. "We'll see about that. Mrs. Lynch is working with the entire staff to do handwriting and drawing analyses of the perpetrator. And Mr. Kennedy is working to uncover who owns the defamatory website. He's our best computer teacher."

He was absolutely correct. Well, I don't know what defamatory meant, so he may have been wrong there. It didn't sound like a real word, but Mr. Kennedy was the best computer teacher in the school. He was also the only one. And the only thing he knew about computers was how to watch YouTube videos about farting cats while he made us read about computers, while sitting in front of a computer. My farts knew more about computers than Mr. Kennedy. And they stink at computers.

I WAS DETERMINED to get to the bottom of both the website and the graffiti mysteries. That night, I rushed through my homework and hopped on my laptop, Googling my fingers and face off, trying to figure out who owned and ran the anti-Butt Hair website. First, I would congratulate them. Then I would turn them in. I needed the Principal off my back once and for all.

My research brought me to something called a Whois search. I typed the website address into the search box and pressed enter. I held my breath, hoping the perpetrator's name would flash in bright lights across my screen. Unfortunately, that was not the case. Some corporation name popped up.

I searched that, too, and found out that it was a company that you could buy website names from. After some research, I learned that you could hide who owned a website, so the bandit was smarter than I had hoped, and remained at large. I guess the good news was that the longer it took me to find this person or persons, the more Principal Buthaire would be bashed in public. He deserved it.

Still, I was disappointed that I came up empty. I was tired of enduring Principal Buthaire's wrath.

7

We needed to make progress on our science project. My dad agreed to drive us to get some parts. We pulled up to the county e-cycle center, which was basically an electronic cemetery, and hopped out. My dad, Ben, and I headed into the giant warehouse through two glass doors. I'd never been there before and wasn't sure what to expect.

The doors opened up to a small, bare room with a dude passed out with his head on the counter. We walked up to him, but he didn't budge.

"Hello?" my dad said, softly.

Nothing. There was a bell on the counter that said, 'Ring for service.' My dad nodded to it.

I smacked my hand down on the bell. The dude sprung up like a pop tart in a toaster, a piece of paper stuck to the drool on his lip. He grabbed the paper and tossed it on the ground and straightened his name badge, which read, 'Glenn'.

"What the-" Glenn smiled, sheepishly. "Er, hello and

welcome to e-cycle, a dignified final resting place for all of your electronics."

"Hello, Glenn," my father said with a chuckle, "Have a good sleep?"

"My apologies, sir. We don't get too many visitors."

Glenn was probably a college kid or maybe a dropout whose dad had some high-up government job.

"Not a problem. My son and his friend here were looking to salvage some old parts for a science project."

Confusion spread across Glenn's face. "Sorry, I-"

"You okay, Glenn?"

"Yeah, dude. You don't look so hot," Ben said, unhelpfully.

"Umm, we don't actually let people take any parts out of here. We only take them in."

"But it's a recycling place. We can help you recycle some parts without you having to do anything," I said. Government red tape, man. It's a downer.

"I just take the stuff in. I don't know what happens to it or where it goes, man."

"Glenn, here's twenty bucks. Mind if we look around and take some stuff home?" my dad asked.

Glenn looked at the twenty dollar bill. "Twenty bucks and I get to go back to sleep?"

"Of course."

Glenn held out his hand for a shake and took the twenty with the other. "Deal."

"Enjoy your nap," I said.

"Straight through those doors," Glenn said, pointing.

"We'll see ourselves out," my dad said.

Once we were inside, my dad said, "He's a real go getter. I think we learned an important lesson today."

"Money talks?" I said.

"No."

"Don't drool when you sleep?" Ben asked.

"Ahh, forget it," my dad said.

There was no organization to the place, just box after box overflowing with stuff and oversized TVs lining the walls.

Ben looked around, eyes wide, and said, "What are we looking for?"

"Oh, yeah." I pulled our shopping list out of my pocket and unfolded the paper. "We need some wiring, a camera lens, a web cam would be good, a microphone, and I think we can buy the microchips online."

We combed through the equipment for at least an hour and left with everything we wanted to find. We were careful not to wake Glenn as we left.

BACK IN SCHOOL, it was like we never left the recycling center. The trash talk between Randy and me was still going full bore. I sat alone at my lab table in science when Randy strolled over.

"How's it going, Davenfart?"

"Fabulous, Warblesucker," I said, making it up on the fly, although you probably figured that out already.

"That doesn't make any sense," Randy said, laughing.

"Neither does your face," I said as cool as possible. A few kids around us laughed. I wasn't sure if it was at me or Randy.

Randy ignored my reply, "How's your project going?" he asked, smugly.

"Crushing it," I said as if it was a ridiculous question. "It's on the verge of changing lives," I said as confidently as possible. "How's yours? Sophie doing all the work as you struggle to find a connection for your one brain cell?"

Randy fake laughed. "Davenfart, you are so outmatched, you're too stupid to even realize how outmatched and stupid you are."

I didn't know what to say, so I decided to go for the 'your breath stinks' attack. Rap style. "Yo, Logan, gimme a beat."

"Huh?" Logan looked at me like I was an idiot.

"A rap beat, dude."

"I'm a nerd. I don't know how to do that," Logan whispered, ashamed.

Randy laughed at me, so I busted out my rhyme, anyway. "Your breath, your breath, your breath is on the attack. I think, I think, I think you need a tick tac. Boom. Mic drop." I wasn't sure if people actually said, "Mic drop," or just dropped it, but whatever.

Sophie walked up, staring at me. Randy took it as an opportunity to stick it to me. "That's hurtful, Austin." He never called me that. Except, apparently when trying to get me in trouble.

Sophie looked at me disapprovingly.

"All right, now," Mr. Gifford called out. "In your seats."

Sophie frowned at me and asked, "What was that about?"

"Nothing. He's just playing to the crowd, acting as usual."

Logan looked over at me and said, "Austin, that was awesome, dude."

I tried to shake my head and gave him hand signals to knock it off. He was not helping.

SCIENCE CLASS CONTINUED LIKE THAT, day after day. Well, without the rapping. I didn't have enough game to pull that off every day. One day, I just couldn't take it anymore. Principal Buthaire was on my case. Derek was on my nerves. And Randy was intolerable as usual.

Randy walked up to my lab table. It was just me. Sophie hadn't arrived yet. I shook my head.

"Are we really going to do this again? Why don't we let our science projects do the talking?"

Randy shook his head. "Nah. We're doing this again." He furrowed his brow. "Hey, what is that?" he asked as he studied my mouth. "Davenfart, are you growing a mustache?" He answered his own question, "No, that's just pudding. Don't worry. One of these days, you'll get a growth spurt. Do kids still think you're in the third grade?"

"Fourth, usually," I said, my face burning red.

I had a pinch of fish food in my hand and the container in the other. I opened my palm and poured as much as I could into my hand and then threw it as hard as I could into Randy's face, so a whopping six miles an hour.

Randy jumped back, his hands rushing to his face. "My

eyes! My eyes! I may never see again. I've never been to the ocean!"

Sophie, Mr. Gifford, and the rest of the class rushed over.

"Oh, stop faking, Randy," I said, not sure how much he was actually faking.

Mr. Gifford ran to the cabinet, grabbed some paper towels and wet them in the sink.

Sophie looked at me and said, "What did you do?" She was quite angry.

"Nothing?" I said, unconvincingly.

"I can't see." Randy held out his hands in front of him, searching to touch something. "All I see is darkness," he said, his lip quivering. "Was that fish food?" Randy started coughing.

"You know it was. You saw me pour it into my hand," I said, knowing he was faking.

Mr. Gifford returned with the wet paper towels.

"I'm allergic to fish," Randy said, like he was about to move on to the afterlife.

"That's all we need...for his head to blow up even bigger," I said.

"Austin!" Sophie yelled.

Mr. Gifford stepped forward and started wiping Randy's eyes with the paper towel. "Hold still, Randy. We'll get you cleaned up and this sorted out."

I looked at Sophie. "He's acting again." I looked at the ingredients on the fish food container and said, "He may be allergic to fish, but this is fish meal and ground brown rice."

"Oh," Randy said, sheepishly. "Still, it hurt."

Mr. Gifford finished cleaning his face.

Randy continued laying it on thick. "Sophie? Is that you?"

Sophie looked at me, fuming. If she got any angrier, steam would have shot from her ears.

Mr. Gifford looked at Randy and said, "Stop playing around, Mr. Warblemacher. Are you okay? Do you need to go to the nurse?"

"No. I'll tough it out," Randy said.

A bunch of kids from Randy's fan club started to clap.

"He's so tough," Ditzy Dayna said.

I just rolled my eyes.

Mr. Gifford looked at me. "Austin, please clean up this mess." He looked around to the rest of the class and said, "Everyone back to your seats. Chop. Chop."

I waited for Mr. Gifford to send me down to the Principal's office. I missed Prince Butt Hair and our stare downs and daily chats about life.

Randy looked over at Mr. Gifford and asked, "Aren't you going to send him to the Principal's office?"

Mr. Gifford said, "What happens in science stays in science. Austin will serve detention with me after school."

Randy's fan club groaned. Apparently, it wasn't good enough for all of the pain and suffering I caused their fishy little friend.

Mr. Gifford leaned in to me and whispered, "You got lucky this time. I don't think you'll be able to lose your cool like that again and get away with it."

SOPHIE REFUSED to respond to my texts, calls, FaceTimes, and yells out my window. They were more for me to release my frustration, because she lived a few miles away, but still, she didn't answer me back and I took that personally.

To make matters worse, pictures of the cardboard

cutouts made it to the website. The interesting part was that the website bandit seemed to take credit for the graffiti artistry. It read, 'Look what I did!' So I guess it wasn't much of a stretch to put two and two together.

"Muahahaha!" I was ecstatic. They were one and the same. I didn't have two cases to solve. Well, I did, but all I had to do was to solve one of them and I would catch both perpetrators, who happened to be the same person. Got me?

My satisfaction didn't last. Reality set back in the next time I saw Sophie. I didn't know what to say most times to Sophie when she didn't hate me. When she was angry, I flat out had nothing. I looked over at her, sitting next to me in music, and said, "I, umm, tried to call you last night."

Sophie looked at me and said, "I know," and turned away.

Mrs. Funderbunk stood in front of the class. "Good morning, class. Mrs. Funderbunk desires to work on resonating. We are going to tighten the drum."

Half the class whispered, "Huh?" Randy was the only one who seemed to know what was going on.

"Does anyone know what that means?" Mrs. Funderbunk asked.

Of course, Randy raised his hand. "The drum is the diaphragm, lungs, and chest. It must remain tight to resonate."

Mrs. Funderbunk beamed. Randy was her star pupil. He beat me out for the lead in the school musical, Santukkah! Don't get me started.

Mrs. Funderbunk said, "Wonderful as always, Randy." She looked out at the rest of us and said, "Flex your muscles around your rib cage and sing like," she closed her eyes and put her finger on her ear like she was in a recording studio and bellowed, "Thiiiiihihihihihiiiiis!"

Since Mrs. Funderbunk was so busy, I leaned into Sophie and said, "Why didn't you call me back?"

Sophie huffed, stood up, and scooted out of our row. She found a new seat in the front row, right next to Randy. Ahhhh, farts.

Mrs. Funderbunk stopped and turned to Sophie. "That doesn't look like tightening the drum, Ms. Rodriguez. What are you doing over there?"

Sophie reddened, "I umm, wanted to try a new seat."

Mrs. Funderbunk said, 'You're going to mess up our harmony," then turned to me and said, "And Austin, why aren't you singing?"

"I, umm, don't feel well."

Somebody called out, "Sophie's mad at him. He's gonna get dumped."

Randy and others laughed. Gulp.

The hurtful comments continued, "Not sure why she likes that nerd to begin with."

Ben turned and yelled at the jerks a few rows behind us, "Like you're cool? You're just jealous."

I pulled Ben back into his seat. "It's okay, Ben. Just chill."

SCIENCE WASN'T any better the next day. I slumped in my seat, staring into the empty fish tank. I looked over at Mr. Gifford and asked, "Where's Boomer?"

"I didn't want to have to tell you this, Austin. He's in fishy heaven. The big fish bowl in the clouds."

All of the drama caught up to me. I could feel the tears welling up inside of me. "What happened?" I said, fighting back the tears.

"I...just can't," Mr. Gifford said and turned away.

"I need to know," I said, forcefully.

"I think he died of starvation," Mr. Gifford said. "I forgot to buy more fish food after you threw it all in Randy's face."

"No! Tell me it isn't true!"

I put my head down and remembered the good times with Boomer. It was mostly just him swimming in circles, but still I think he enjoyed them.

I heard Sophie put her books down on the lab table. I looked over at her and sat up. "Hey," I said out of habit.

"Umm, hi." Sophie said, picking at her nails.

"What's wrong?" I asked. Besides everything. She seemed nervous.

"Nothing," she said, unconvincingly. "Totally unrelated, but have you been to your locker since music?"

"No," I said, confused. "Why?"

"I...thought I saw...Butt Hair."

"In my locker?"

"Well, no. Near your locker."

I looked at her like she needed medical attention. "Thank you for that useful information. I'll be on the lookout the next time I see Butt Hair by your locker."

"Great," Sophie said. "That would be very helpful."

I shook my head, not sure what the heck was going on.

I figured it out at the end of the day after I made it to my locker, Sophie's big concern. After the final bell, I stood in front of my locker, dialed in the combo, and opened it. I pulled out my jacket and a folded-up piece of paper popped out of my locker. I tried to snatch it out of the air, but given my lack of coordination and athletic prowess, I missed badly, and smacked my knuckles on the locker with a thud.

"Oww!" I said, shaking my hand out.

I turned around to see what just flew out of my locker. I didn't remember anything shaped like that and certainly not just sitting on top of my jacket. I scanned the floor and found the note sitting at the feet of none other than Randy Warblemacher and two of his teammates, David Betz and Jonathan Webber.

Randy looked at the paper and then at me and said with a smile, "What do we have here?" Randy picked up the folded paper and examined it. "There are no hearts so it can't be a love note. Plus, who would love you anyway?"

I walked up to Randy calmly. "Thanks for picking that up for me." I tried to grab it out of his hand, but he had too firm a grip on it, and my fingers slipped off.

"Not so fast," Randy said, his buddies laughing.

"Give it back. It's mine," I said, standing not so patiently in front of him.

Randy said, "I found it on the floor. It's public property."

"Give it to me," I said, reaching for it again.

"What are you going to do about it?" Randy asked.

It was a good question. A crowd was starting to form as I struggled for the note. Randy held it above my head. Since he was a basketball player, I had no shot at reaching it, but I struggled for it anyway. I even threw in a few lame attempts at jumping. They were more like nerd hops, but even more stupid.

David Betz boxed me out as Randy began reading, "Dear Austin- I'm sorry to have to tell you this in a letter." Randy looked up at me and said, "Oh, that doesn't sound good." He laughed and continued reading, "I'm breaking up with you." Randy looked at me again. "It's about time. Nobody knew what she was thinking."

Emotions swirled within me. I felt tears starting to build up.

Randy said through laughter, "Oh, is baby Austin gonna cry?" David and Jon joined him, laughing and pointing at me.

Just Charles walked up to my side and said, "Just walk away, dude. It's not worth it."

I managed to say, "You're such a jerk," before Just Charles ushered me away from the idiots.

"You don't want your letter?" Randy said, holding it out.

I rushed out of the school and hurried down the sidewalk and the line of buses. Dozens of kids rushed to catch their buses.

Just Charles said, "Dude, where are you going?"

"I need to be alone," I said, wiping my eyes with my sleeve. "Thanks for the help back there." I didn't dare look at him.

I looked across the sidewalk to see Ben and Sammie looking at me through the bus window as the doors closed.

Ben mouthed, "Where are you going?"

I ignored him and kept walking. I probably lived more than two miles from the school, but I'd rather walk than be around anyone. I certainly wasn't in the mood to answer any questions about what happened.

∼

THAT NIGHT, I wanted nothing to do with anyone. Well, anyone but Sophie. My parents didn't know what was wrong until my brother found out from his hoops buddies/idiots. Derek sang like a canary, hoping to get me in trouble for leaving him at school. I didn't care.

My parents tried to get me to talk, but I would rather spend the night alone in my room. I didn't even have the strength to work on my science fair project.

I lay on my bed and mustered up enough strength in my thumb to unlock my phone and call Sophie. The profile pic of us together at Frank's Pizza popped up as the phone dialed and crushed my soul. I held my breath as it rang. No answer. I FaceTimed her. No answer. I texted her. Delivered, but no response. Not even the typing bubble thing. I had been dumped by a locker note and didn't even get a chance to read it to understand why.

I didn't put it past Randy to make it all up, but the fact that Sophie was so anxious when she asked me if I had been to my locker deflated my hope that the breakup was all a lie. Saustin (our couple name given to us by Nerd Nation) was no more. I threw the phone across my bed. It landed with a smack and skidded across my night table.

As I lay in the fetal position, sucking my thumb, my phone beeped, signaling that a text had arrived. I rolled over to my night stand and slapped my limp arm on the table, searching for the phone. I didn't have the energy to actually look. I knocked over half the stuff on the night stand before finding my phone.

I held the phone in front of my face and said "What do you want?"

It didn't answer. It could be rude like that sometimes.

I opened one eye and typed in my password. I half hoped it was Sophie and half hoped it wasn't. I wanted to know what the heck was going on, but I didn't want any more bad news. Although I couldn't think of what could be worse than Sophie dumping me.

It was from Ben. There was an update to the website.

I typed back, 'I don't care. About anything. I give up. Randy wins. Buthaire wins. Austin Davenfart- super loser'

I dropped the phone onto the bed next to me. Another text rang. Ugh. I picked it up and checked it. It was Ben again.

'Are you okay?' Ben wanted to know.

Was he serious? 'I'm going to join the circus. Are there even any circuses to join anymore?"

'That bad, huh?'

'No, I've always wanted to join the circus. Introducing Austin Davenfart, middle school clown!'

8

I waited until everyone in my family was in bed for the night before emerging from my cave of despair. I didn't realize lying around doing nothing could make me so hungry. Plus, I had to pee. I hadn't cried too much, so I was still close to fully hydrated.

I tiptoed past my parents' bedroom, made a quick pit stop in the bathroom, and then continued my search for nourishment. I made my way into the kitchen without any trouble and flipped on the light over the oven. The last thing I needed was to lose a toe jamming it on a piece of furniture. If Sophie didn't want to be with me with all my toes, she certainly wouldn't want me with nine.

The fridge lights blasted my face like I was staring at the sun after emerging from the underworld of darkness. I searched the shelves, peeking between my fingers. I scanned past a jar of pickles, mustard, some weird concoction that looked like it was well past expiration (unless food is supposed to look neon green), and stopped dead on the maraschino cherries. My lip quivered as I tried to hold in the emotion. Sophie loved cherries. When we got ice cream together, she would get like twelve of them. After, her lips would be all red.

I grabbed the jar of cherries and picked them up. I held them close to me.

"Sophie. Sweet Sophie. Why?" I said, through tears.

It was all I had left of her. I sobbed for what seemed like an hour, just hugging the cherries in my arms. It was at that point that I realized there was no way I was going to school the next morning. If cherries could make me splutter like a baby after his doll was taken away, I couldn't risk actually seeing her. I could go full baby and need a diaper or something. I embarrassed myself enough on good days. Who knew what could happen on my worst day?

But how could I get out of school? I kissed the jar of cherries (I may have petted and talked to them, too. May have.) and put it back on the shelf next to the mustard. My eyes caught the neon green concoction.

I was going to have to sell my parents on letting me stay home from school. They weren't the type of people to just let me stay home whenever I wanted. Derek, maybe. But he had the family butt chin and they loved him more because of it. They won't admit it, but I know it's true.

There were a lot of ways I could try to get out of school, but there was only one fool-proof method. Puke. And lots of it. The question was, how bad did I want it? I could make up a mixture of gross-looking foods, a puke stew, if you will. Or I could go all in and actually regurgitate preferably very chunky and foul-smelling food.

I picked up the neon green jar, not sure if I should touch it without a biohazard suit on. I studied the seemingly alien matter, wondering if it was Kryptonite. Whatever it was, I was sure it wasn't on the periodic chart.

There was no way I was eating that and regurgitating it to get out of school. I'd rather run away and actually join the circus. Plus, while disgusting, given its pulsating green color, I was concerned my parents either wouldn't believe that it was actual puke or that they would and rush me to a government test facility, never to be seen again.

I was going to have to make some tweaks. I grabbed a plastic container from the recycling bin and put it in the sink. I took a deep breath and psyched myself up. I slipped on my mother's yellow rubber kitchen gloves and picked up the green glob jar. The pulsing seemed to quicken, which caused my own pulse to race. This thing seemed to have some sort of intelligent life to it, sensing its own doom.

After staring at the jar for a moment, I whispered, "It's now or never, Davenport." I inhaled deeply and held it as I struggled to open the jar. The top twisted slowly and then fully off. I quickly poured it into the bigger container, the glob of goo splattering in the container with a slap. I exhaled, thankful that it didn't take some sort of humanistic form and eat or dispose of me, or both.

Then it was time for Austin, the artist, to emerge. I needed to turn a pile of alien poo into human puke. No easy task. The problem was that my artistic skills were pitiful. I could barely draw stick figures. First, we needed to deal with the coloring. That was easy enough. A cup of milk turned the neon green into a pale green, definitely more puke-like. I surmised that the milk proteins also neutralized the pulsation, which took my fear meter down by about a million.

I stared into the mix with a frown. "It still needs something," I whispered to myself. "What does every good fake pile of puke need?" I thought for a moment and then it hit me. No, not the glob of fake puke. An idea. Every good fake pile of puke needed chunks.

I walked back to the fridge, opened it, and scanned the contents. There was nothing even remotely chunky. And whatever I chose, had to be something my parents thought I would eat. I closed the fridge in a huff and walked over to the pantry. I looked up and down and all around. And then, as if a beam of sunlight broke through the clouds from heaven, a can of chicken soup seemed to glow in front of me.

"Ha, ha!" I laughed, a little too loud. I closed the pantry door slowly and walked back to the sink.

I pulled out the utility drawer and slowly and quietly, I searched for a can opener. I grabbed it and slipped it out, and pushed the drawer closed. I sliced the top open and slowly poured the soup into the slime container. It looked good. Well, it looked like disgusting puke, but that's what I was going for.

I grabbed the puke container in one hand and the empty soup can in the other. I dropped the can in the recycling bin on the way out of the kitchen and tip toed to the bathroom. Without turning the light on, I closed the door and found a solid hiding place for my puke under the sink behind cabinet doors. I put a small towel over the top of it and closed the doors. My puke plan was ready to go.

I woke up thirty minutes earlier than normal. I needed to beat my sister into the bathroom. Her bus came earlier than ours, so she always got dibs on the first shower. I rolled out of bed. My stomach actually felt sick. I think I was nervous to lie to my mother and also that if it didn't work, I would have to go to school and see Sophie. She hadn't called or texted me back. And I didn't hear any yelling throughout the night on the off chance she decided to respond to my own yelling.

I opened my door and ran down the hall to the bathroom, nearly knocking over a potted plant in the corner. I fake wretched as I passed my parents' bedroom, making sure to make the 'hwulah' extra loud. I slammed the door, desperate to gain my parents' attention. You know, like usual. You would think that being the baby would mean something in the Davenport family, but as you know, it's all about the butt chin and this chin o' mine ain't got no butt. I did once try to create my own butt chin with some crazy glue and wood clamps, but unfortunately, I was unsuccessful.

Back to the story. I opened the cabinet and pulled out the puke, which seemed to have gotten more potent overnight. The milk was nice and warm and the chicken spoiling by the second. I did a quick fist pump and lifted up the toilet seat with authority, the porcelain clanging.

I made sure to time my puke sounds to the pouring of my concoction. "Hwulaaaaah!" I yelled and then poured. "Hwulaaaaahaaaahoooola!" The puke purée splattered around the bowl. It looked so good, I almost celebrated. "Focus, Davenport. Focus," I whispered.

I heard a knock on the door and my mother say, "Austin, is that you? Are you okay?"

"No," I said like an old man who had just been run over by a stampede of hyenas. If you've never heard an old man talk after being stampeded by any jungle animal, let me just tell you, it doesn't sound good.

"Did you throw up?"

Didn't you hear my fabulous performance? "Yes," I said, weakly, barely clinging to life.

"Open the door."

"Okay," I said, reaching for the handle. I unlocked the door and then realized I still held the puke container in my other hand.

The door knob twisted and the door pushed open. I pushed back quickly in a panic. "Hold on. The cabinet door is open."

I tore open the cabinet and threw the container under the sink and then shut the door again. I stepped back and pulled the door open.

My mother stood in the doorway, a look of concern on her face.

"Mommy," I whined. Yes, I was laying it on thick. "I... don't feel well."

"Oh, baby, what's the matter?"

"I didn't feel well yesterday, but I was hungry late last night. I probably shouldn't have eaten, but Gammy always says that chicken soup helps when you're sick." Yes, I was bringing my Gammy into this.

My mother stepped past me and inspected the puke in the bowl. I peeked around her to see how it looked. I was pleased. I held my breath, waiting for her response.

"Hmm," she said. Uh, oh.

I needed to get rid of it quick. "Ugh, the smell. Can you flush it?" I fake wretched.

My mother leaned over and pressed the handle. My fabulous creation disappeared without so much as a good-bye. Godspeed and thank you, I thought to myself.

My mother looked over to me and started to clap. She said, "Excellent performance. And that was a nice concoction, but frankly I think you could've done better. Mr. Gifford would've been disappointed."

"What do you mean?" I moaned. My heart raced. I instinctively knew I had been caught red-handed and yellow-puked, but I wasn't ready to give up.

"Austin, come on. You have two older siblings and a mother who tried to get out of school once or twice in her life."

"Really?" I didn't know that about my mom.

"Yep."

I wasn't ready to give up just yet. "I'm not faking."

My mother cocked her head and smiled. "Your theatrics were certainly better than mine, but that wasn't puke."

"Ah, man. How did you know I was faking?" I asked.

"I'm a mom. It's my job. Plus, you didn't leave a soup bowl in the sink."

I shrugged. "It was 4 a.m. Mistakes were made. Did you buy the chunky soup at least?"

"Not in the slightest," my mom said, laughing. "And you owe me $1.99 for wasting the soup."

"Aww, really? Nobody eats that soup anyway."

"Okay, then you owe me for the milk."

I took a deep breath. "Okay."

"So, what's going on?"

"Mom, I just don't want to go to school today. Sophie

dumped me. Randy embarrassed me. I just can't take any more."

My mother rubbed my back. "I understand, sweetie. I'm sorry to hear about all that. I wish you would've told us more yesterday. You wouldn't have had to go through this all alone."

"All alone...without Sophie," I whimpered.

MY MOTHER WAS THE BEST. She let me stay home anyway and even told Derek that I did puke. I decided to attempt to be productive rather than wallow in self-pity and tears, although there was still some of that. I sat in the den, dismantling an old video camera. I needed to harvest the microphone to enable the voice activation for our robot. Plastic parts, screws, washers, and wires were just about everywhere except where they were supposed to be.

My mother was in the kitchen, reading. It was nice being in my house while it was quiet. Usually, Derek was complaining about something, ordering me around, or chasing me. If it wasn't that, Leighton was freaking out about ridiculous high school drama: hair, boys, clothes she wasn't allowed to wear. Repeat.

I was concentrating on unscrewing the microphone with a teeny, tiny screwdriver that even Santa's Elves would have a tough time using. The phone rang like a fire engine's siren on full blast.

"Ahhh!" I yelled, parts flying everywhere.

My mother said from the other room, "It's the school, but I already told them you weren't going in." She sighed. "I wonder what your brother did." She turned on her happy voice, "Hello?...Oh, Principal Buthaire...Yes, Austin wasn't feeling well...He'll be okay...I appreciate your concern, but really, it's not necessary...Well, no...He doesn't have any web design experience. Not that I know of. Do you need help with the school website? I'm sure he could learn...Okay... Have a good day."

My mom hung up the phone and walked into the den. "That was weird."

"What happened?"

"Principal Buthaire asked if you were okay, but I think he wanted to find out if you had any web design experience. Why the heck would he want to know that?"

I exhaled, frustrated. "Because somebody created an anti-butt hair website."

"Butt hair? What are you talking about?"

Oops. "Oh, we all call him Prince Butt Hair." I tried to say it as nonchalantly as possible. I didn't dare tell her I made it up.

"To his face?" She asked, flabbergasted.

"Of course not. Only behind his back," I said, like that was okay. "Or really behind his butt hair," I said, holding back laughter. I apparently was the only one who found it funny.

"Isn't that lovely?" My mother asked rhetorically. "I can't say that I approve of that, even though he is a dweeb. Do kids still use the word dweeb?"

"No, not at all."

"Well, he is one. And they should."

~

My mother wouldn't let me stay home another day, so I had to suck it up and take whatever ridicule was set to come my way. I'm sure Randy hadn't forgotten what had happened in the whopping one day I was gone. And I had two classes with Sophie. She probably wouldn't sit near me in music, but she was still my lab partner in science. There was no avoiding her. Not that I wanted to. I wanted to be her boyfriend again in the worst way, but that was over. The awkwardness of it all probably meant our friendship was, too.

As I stuffed my books in my locker as fast as I could, hoping everyone would just leave me alone, I felt hot breath on my neck. I thought it was Luke. We call him Luke the Lurker. Sometimes he would just appear out of nowhere, but wouldn't say anything. I felt his presence, so I turned around. It was a big mistake. As if my life was not already swirling around in the toilet, Amanda Gluskin apparently found out I was a free man and wanted to make her move.

"You never texted me," she said, her lower lip protruding sadly.

"Yeah, umm, things haven't been going my way lately."

"Are you sure? 'Cause the way I see it, this could be the best thing that ever happened to us."

To us? Uh, oh. I was in trouble. I needed to think fast. "Well, you see, Amanda, I hate to tell you this, but...we can never be together."

Her face dropped. "Why not?" she whispered.

I hadn't figured that out yet. I had to tread carefully. She could blow at any second. And then I got it. I had to give her someone else to chase. "My brother, Derek. I think he has a crush on you. There's like a bro code, you know? I couldn't do that to him."

Amanda's face glowed. "Really?" she asked, excitedly.

"You don't look upset." I should've been happy, but I wasn't.

"Why would I be? I'd rather date him than you. Do you know where he is for first period?"

She made me feel really good about myself. I guess I deserved it. Looking back, it wasn't the nicest thing to do. I was just in a funk and any time I could get back at my brother, I took it.

Advisory was pretty uneventful. I stared at my desk during the morning announcements, careful to avoid any eye contact with anyone. I was miserable and didn't want to talk to anyone or take junk from anyone. It was easy to pretend it hadn't happened when I was at home and engulfed in my science project, but back in school, the hurt came rushing back as soon as the stupid yellow bus pulled up at our stop.

Just Charles whispered, "Dude, are you okay? I tried to FaceTime you like seven times."

I continued to stare at my desk. "I don't know. I don't want to be here."

"And what the heck were you doing talking to Amanda Gluskin? Every time she looks at me, I think she's gonna eat me."

I looked over at him. "I know, right? She kinda asked me...out."

"What?" Just Charles said a little too loud. "That's a terrible idea. Did you see what she did to Mr. Muscalini? He runs every time he sees her. And he's a bodybuilder."

"It wasn't my idea. It was hers. I told her that Derek liked her so we couldn't be together."

"Dude, that's an even worse idea. What are you gonna do when she finds out that he doesn't actually like her?"

I scratched my head as a sense of dread surged through my body. "I hadn't thought of that."

And then the Speaker of Doom interrupted us. I stood

up before I even heard what was being said. A few kids around me chuckled.

Of course, I was right. The Speaker of Doom blasted the words, "Is Austin Davenport in school today?"

My teacher, Mrs. Callahan said, "Yes," and rolled her eyes at me.

"Please send him down to Principal Buthaire's office."

At that point, I should've just swung by there every morning after I got off the bus, to see if there were any detention passes waiting for me. Prince Butt Hair's vendetta against me had gotten that intense.

I made my way down to The Butt Crack. I sat in the chair across from Principal Buthaire's desk, which had his smug face and the rest of him seated behind it.

"I noticed you were out of school, sick, yesterday," Principal Buthaire said with a disapproving tone and a raised eye brow.

"Yes, I was umm, under the weather."

"Do you have a doctor's note?"

"No. but my mother called. You spoke to her, too, so I'm not sure why I'm here."

"I did speak to her. You're here because interestingly enough, there was another update to the website."

"What website, sir?" I asked. I wasn't in the mood to make it easy on him.

"You know what website I'm talking about. The one about me."

"You have your own website? Why does a Principal need his own website?"

"Stop playing coy. I didn't make the website. I need to find out who. Whom? Is it whom?"

"I'm in sixth grade. How the heck should I know?"

Principal Buthaire straightened his glasses and leaned

forward. "Never you mind. My point is- you were out of school, sick, and there was also a rather significant update to the website, taking place at the exact same time."

"I don't know how to prove that it wasn't me, but it wasn't," I said, shrugging.

"Do you know what I have to say about that?" Principal Buthaire said, with excitement.

"Detention?" I said, defeated.

Prince Butt Hair's face morphed from elation to disappointment. "Detention," he said, deflated.

I didn't even know what I got detention for. Maybe it was for existing without Principal approval. I can't keep track of all the rules anymore. "I can't do anything around here without getting detention. Is it against the rules to breathe yet?"

Principal Buthaire narrowed his eyes at me. "Not yet, but I'm working on it."

Military school was sounding better by the minute. I needed to figure the whole thing out. It was beyond ridiculous.

MUSIC WAS A HORROR SHOW. I made it through by laying under my chair, sucking my thumb in the fetal position. It was the only time I had ever wanted to be struck by the Speaker of Doom and summoned down to the Butt Crack. Mrs. Funderbunk insisted on singing love songs.

Sophie, of course, kept her new seat near Randy. I tried not to look, but I couldn't keep my eyes off of her. It was partly because she was so pretty, but also partly because I wanted her to know how much she hurt my feelings. She kept checking over her shoulder, nervously. I didn't know what to make of that.

Science wasn't any better. In fact, it was worse. I sat next to Sophie. All the things I wanted to say to her when I called her the night before remained stubbornly inside. I was too nervous, too embarrassed to talk to her with other kids around. She didn't make any effort to talk to me, either.

I spent half the period ignoring taunts from Randy while Sophie wasn't looking. He had apparently not forgotten about the note he intercepted. I wondered if he had it framed by his bed so he could enjoy my misery every day and night.

I spent the other half of the period agonizing over wanting to talk to her, but not actually wanting to talk to her. Middle school is complicated. I don't know what you want me to tell you. There was no easy fix.

After school, Ben and I spent some time coding our project and giving voice commands. YouTube was very helpful in learning how to do a lot of it. I had no idea how people got anything done before the Internet.

We sat in my room, working. The longer we worked, the more tired I got, and the less I was able to keep my mind off of Principal Buthaire and the website.

"I don't think I can take two and a half more years of this. There are five hundred kids in the school, most of them idiots, and I'm the one who gets blamed for everything. Me! It's not fair."

"Did you figure anything out about the website?"

"I'm making some progress. I know that we can track the domain name to the IP address, but I need to figure out who owns the IP address."

"Sounds fun," Ben said.

"It's a blast. Like I have time for all of this."

"How does Principal Buthaire have time for it?"

"No idea. Maybe this is all he does. Do you think his wife actually likes him?"

"No. That's impossible," Ben said, laughing.

I looked at my watch. "We'd better head over to the library and get started with the 3D printer."

That night we went to the library to build the exoskeleton of our robot hand. It would house all of the loose wires, motors, and computer chips, and protect the wheels. It was the skin that was going to cover the guts. We spent all night designing it. It took until closing time. We set it to print overnight. By the time the library opened the next morning, the piece would be complete, and we could start putting everything together.

THE NEXT MORNING, I felt Luke lurking. I turned around, my fists in the air, just in case it was Amanda. Once I saw it was Luke, I pretended I was just going to give him a fist bump.

"Hey," I said, with a nod.

Luke was missing. I told you, he was like a wizard or something. Then I realized he just ducked from my fist.

"Hey, just wanted to check and see if you were all right?"

"I don't know how to answer that," I said.

"I hear ya. I wouldn't know what to say if I were you either, after I'd heard that Sophie was dating Randy Warblemacher," he said, nonchalantly.

My heart imploded. I fell to the ground.

I tried to keep my eyes open, but couldn't. I saw a bright light at the end of a tunnel. I walked through the tunnel toward the light. Silhouettes appeared in the distance. As I approached, I could see my great grandfather, Poppy, and my dog, Doggie Davenport (that's what you get when you let baby Leighton name the dog), both of whom died a few years prior.

I felt Luke shaking me. I heard his distant voice, "Austin! Austin! Are you okay? Wake up!"

The light started to fade. "No, Poppy. Doggie...Come back," I whispered.

I opened my eyes to see Luke, Just Charles, Ben, Dr. Dinkledorf, and Nurse Nova standing over me. Nurse Nova leaned in, her blonde hair tickling my nose, and took my pulse as she checked her watch.

"Are you okay? "Nurse Nova asked.

"It depends," I whispered.

"On what?"

I had no interest in getting into it. "Physically, I'm fine."

"Can you get up?" Nurse Nova asked.

"Yes," I said. But did I want to? I wasn't sure of that.

Mr. Muscalini walked up with a frown. Oh, God. I didn't need that. He looked at me with a raised eye brow.

"Looks like somebody needs some motivation," Mr. Muscalini said. He flexed his bicep and continued, "Well, here it comes."

"No, I'm good. Feeling great. Help me up, please."

Mr. Muscalini didn't seem to care. "We're the Cherry Avenue Gophers. And that means something, Davenport."

"Okay, boys. Help him up," Dr. Dinkledorf said

Ben and Luke grabbed my hands and pulled.

Mr. Muscalini continued, "It means that we might not be the biggest..." He looked at his bicep. "But we could be. But even if we aren't, like you, we're fighters. Gophers will fight to the death to protect their tunnels and their food from intruders! Are you with me?"

"Sir, I think we need to look into new mascot options. I think you're the only one that identifies with gophers."

"Nonsense. Dinkledorf is a Gopher through and through. Isn't that right?"

"We're the Gophers? I thought we were some sort of pheasant. No?"

Mr. Muscalini shook his head in disgust.

IT TOOK SOME TIME, but I thought things were getting better with Sophie. She and I could communicate somewhat in science. I mainly spoke in grunts and nods, but sometimes I got some actual words in. It was nowhere near back to normal, but they were getting better. As for Randy, things were as difficult as ever.

Well, I thought things were okay with Sophie until one day, I was late to science. I walked into the classroom to see Randy sitting in my seat next to Sophie at our lab table. I took a deep breath and exhaled. I walked over to Randy and put my books on the table in front of him.

"You're in my seat," I said, firmly.

Typical Randy, he ignored me.

I looked at Sophie and said, "Your bo- your buhull-bahoy-"

"Davenfart, are you having a seizure or something?" Randy asked without concern.

I continued without acknowledging Randy. "Your friend who's a boy is in my seat and I want him out of it."

The bell rang. Mr. Gifford called out, "All right class, settle in."

Randy got up and petted Sophie's hand as he walked away. "Until later, my love."

I nearly threw up in my mouth. I looked over at Sophie and said, "Thanks for the help. Not." I got her good.

"It doesn't have to be this way," she whispered.

"No, it doesn't. But don't blame it on me. You dumped me and chose the biggest bully in the whole school as your blah- your blahah- your friend who's a boy."

"Austin-"

"Don't talk to me unless it involves school, okay?"

"I still want to be friends," she said, quietly.

"My calculations suggest that's fairly impossible."

"Fairly impossible? What does that even mean?"

"What does any of it mean?" I said softly and looked up at Mr. Gifford as he started the class.

Not only had I lost to Randy Warblemacher, he had broken my beautiful mind. I was cracking up.

9

I didn't realize that after building a voice-activated robot from recycled parts, the most difficult part of the project had yet to come: creating the project board.

Ben had brought over a giant tri-fold poster board. We were going to show our designs, pictures of the robot in various stages of development, and list its capabilities and potential uses.

"You gotta hold it in place. Push on it hard," Ben said.

"I am!" I squeezed my index finger and thumb together as hard as I could.

After about a minute, Ben said, "That should be good."

I let go. But I did not, in fact, actually let go.

Ben said, "That should be good."

"What the-" I tried to pull my fingers off the board, but they wouldn't budge.

"Dude, get my dad," I said, defeated.

Ben left for a minute while I sat there helpless, glued to the board.

Ben returned with my father, both of them laughing.

"Really, Austin?" my dad said, barely getting the words out.

"It's not funny," I said, half mad, half laughing against my will.

"You can build a robot, but you glue yourself to the project?" my dad said, surprised.

Ben said, "Nerd problems."

I shook my head. It just wasn't fair.

THE SCIENCE FAIR took place over three days. The first day was for set up. Day two was for exhibitions. Kids, parents, teachers, and members of the local community would go around to each project to learn more about them. The final day was judgement day. Oral presentations would be made to a team of judges and prizes would be awarded for best project and best presentation.

My dad was able to take us to school to drop our project off. Ben and I headed in with our poster board and backpacks. We wanted to check in and get settled before bringing in our robot.

As I entered the atrium, I saw Mr. Gifford. Ben and I walked as coordinated as two nerds could walk while carrying the presentation board. We headed over to Mr. Gifford.

"Hey, Mr. Gifford. Where should we go?"

Mr. Gifford shrugged, seemingly upset. "I'm not in charge of the science fair anymore. Principal Buthaire took over. You'll have to check in with him and get your booth location."

"I'm guessing mine will be in the detention room."

Mr. Gifford cracked a smile. "Good luck. I'll be in a bit later to see everything."

"Thanks," I said, as we made our way to the gym.

There was a line to get into the gym. It was the only time us science geeks ever wanted to get in there. Principal Buthaire and Mrs. Wendell, one of the main office staff, stood behind a table, checking in kids. The place was littered with giant poster boards, some even taller than the students.

My pulse started to quicken once we got up to the front of the table. I tried to inch my way over to Mrs. Wendell. While she wasn't exactly the nicest person I'd ever met, she didn't have a vendetta against me like Principal Buthaire did. Unfortunately, Principal Buthaire saw me after he was done checking in Krista Vreeland.

"Ahh, Mr. Davenport. So good to see you," Principal Buthaire said.

I knew better than to think he was serious. "Good morning. We'd like to check in." I wanted to keep it straight and to the point. He couldn't give me detention for being late, his go-to excuse. I didn't want to give him any other reasons.

He scanned a paper list. "Project?" he asked. "Mechanical robot," he said, without waiting for my answer.

I didn't tell him what I was doing. I looked at our presentation board and it was folded so nobody could see what it was. How did he know what I was doing? Could Mr. Gifford have told him even though he knew it was a secret?

"How did you know that, sir? I don't remember telling you."

"I have my sources, Mr. Davenport. You are table forty two. There's another interesting robot project you might want to have a look at. Enjoy." He actually seemed happy, which meant something was wrong for the rest of us and probably me.

"Thank you," I said and then whispered to Ben, "Hurry up. Let's get out of here before he realizes he didn't punish me for not combing my hair perfectly."

"What was that all about?" Ben asked.

"I don't know, but I don't feel good about it."

Of course, Principal Buthaire had sent us to the farthest corner of the earth for our science fair booth. I needed an IV drip by the time we got there. After I took a nap to reenergize from the long journey, Ben and I set up our project board at our table in East Siberia, next to the utility closet that usually sounded like it was going to explode.

On our way back to the car to get our robot, Ben and I admired some of the science projects that were already set up. The competition looked solid, but it was nothing we couldn't handle. I was pretty pleased with what we accomplished.

Some looked pretty cool. There was a hovercraft and some remote-controlled cars. There were also some very questionable projects. I saw at least three volcanos. Why, people? Why? There was also a project attempting to answer the age-old question of why really old people smell. Another explored the idea of human cheese. Middle school is filled with a bunch of weirdos, I tell ya.

Mark Schottland hypothesized what penguins would need to fly, which sounded kind of cool. And the winner of the most ridiculous project we saw came from Ditzy Dayna and Kimmy Akira who apparently attempted to prove that Taylor Swift and Ke$ha are the same person with multiple personality disorder.

I wasn't sure how they were actually going to prove that. Both singers were invited to the science fair. It was most likely that neither of them would show up. Still, if one did, it wouldn't prove the other didn't exist. And if both did show up for some crazy reason, it would prove them wrong. But it was at least looking like I could beat both of them, so I was happy about that.

I really only cared about beating Randy, though. I mean, winning the whole thing would be really cool, but I was out for revenge in the worst way. And I had scienced my face off in order to pull it off. I mean, how many kids in middle school can code a robot they built from scratch and control it using voice commands? I was going to win, unless Principal Buthaire cheated. So, I was probably going to lose. Maybe that's what he was planning.

Ben and I returned from the car and carried our robot into the gym under a blanket. We still wanted it to remain a secret. We each had both hands on it and walked slowly as if it could crumble into a thousand pieces with even the slightest misstep, which was entirely possible.

And then my eyes almost made my hands let go. Across the gym, I saw Randy and Sophie readying their project. It was a giant robot hand! My face flushed red. I thought my blood would literally boil. That's what Principal Buthaire knew!

Ben must have seen me nearly convulsing and said, "Hey, what's wrong?"

I couldn't speak. All I could do was nod in evil's direction.

"Are you kidding me?" Ben screamed across the gym. We just never had any good luck in gym. Even when it was science-related. It was like nerd Kryptonite.

I regained my voice, "Let's just put this down before I smash it."

Ben nodded and we hurried over to our table. We placed

our robot down safely and slumped into the two chairs at our booth.

"How could Randy have found out what we were doing? Or did he come up with this on his own?" Ben asked.

The only two people who could've told anyone were Mr. Gifford and the most obvious choice, my brother, the butt-chinned bandit. He had given away more of my secrets than I could even count, and I was pretty good at math.

"I'm guessing it was my idiot brother. What else is new? I did tell Mr. Gifford, too."

"We should ask him just to see."

"Maybe Randy will tell us. I want to go see what he's got," I said. Interacting with Randy was always a risk. There was a 50% chance he would embarrass me. And there was a 50% chance I would embarrass myself.

"Okay, he's there now. But Sophie's there," Ben said.

I shrugged. "Let's do this."

Ben and I walked over to Randy's booth, which of course, was dead center in the gym down the main aisle. Nobody was going to miss it. Whatever buzz it generated would be for everyone, including the judges, to see.

Randy and Sophie looked up at us as we arrived. Randy chuckled to himself. Sophie started to fidget with her shirt.

"Interesting project, Randy," I said, trying to remain calm, but not sure if I was pulling it off. "Where did you come up with the topic?" I pointed to his poster board, which had a giant robot hand in the middle of it.

Randy ran his fingers through his hair. "I've been inter-ested in robotics for a long time." He looked at Sophie. "And I like to help people, so I found a way to join the two together."

"That's really interesting. Something confuses me, though."

"That's not surprising," Randy responded.

I ignored his comment. "Don't you find it odd that we have nearly the same exact project?"

Randy paused for a second. "You did a robotics project, too? It's a really interesting topic. I didn't have time to see what your project was all about. What a coincidence."

"Yeah. A big one. Like almost too big to be a coincidence."

Randy frowned at me. "What are you trying to say?"

"I'm not trying to say anything. I said it was too big of a coincidence to actually be one."

"Are you saying I cheated?"

"No, but you just did."

"That's the stupidest thing your face has ever said."

I laughed, "You're wrong again, Randy. My face has said much dumber stuff than this."

Randy stepped toward me. "And I didn't say I cheated."

"You did. You said very clearly, 'I cheated.' You've said it twice actually."

"Hey, you just said it," Randy responded quickly.

"I was quoting you!"

Sophie stepped forward. "Boys, enough. Austin, just walk away."

I shook my head at her, disappointed. "It's always my fault, right Sophie?"

She didn't answer. She just huffed and turned away. I watched her as I started to leave.

Sophie looked at Randy and said, "Let's clean some of this stuff up." She picked up a notebook and reached for Randy's backpack.

"No! Don't touch that-" Randy said, alarmed. He paused and said, "I, umm, have an art project in there for my mom's birthday."

"Okay," Sophie said, surprised. She placed the notebook back on the table.

I thought about making a run for it and stealing his backpack. I really wanted to see what he was hiding in there, but I figured Randy would catch me in like two steps and pummel me for being a thief, so I decided against it.

ABOUT AN HOUR LATER, I bumped into Sophie on the way back from the bathroom. Unfortunately, it wasn't Max's. That was too far from the gym. I had to use the regular smelly school one.

I couldn't let it go. As I walked toward her, I asked Sophie pointedly, "You really want to be friends, huh?"

Sophie frowned. "What do you mean? Of course, I do."

"You keep saying that, but everything you do says the opposite. Where did you get your project idea?"

"Randy came up with it. What's this all about?"

"We have the same project. Something's fishy." Admittedly, it was a poor choice of words since Sophie basically dumped me for throwing fish food in Randy's face, but it was too late.

"Real funny, Austin," Sophie said, angry.

"It's not funny at all. Randy stole my idea. He's a cheater. And you and I will never be friends." I turned and walked away.

10

W ith the science project complete and set up for the exhibition, I had time that night at home to work on finding out who was behind the anti-Butt Hair website. I think most people are against butt hair in general, so it was a pretty long list of suspects. I put a 'Do not disturb' sign on my bedroom door and Googled my fingers off. My butt hurt from sitting in the chair so long.

I was more prepared for my research session than the time I spent sleeping on Sophie's front lawn. Do you remember that? It was when my idiot brother tried to take down the school dance. I had all the essentials. Chips, pretzels, cookies, juice boxes, water, and a little bit of soda, which my parents don't let me drink a lot of. That being said, I didn't wear a diaper like I did at Sophie's. I swore I would never do that again. And I don't want to talk about it now, thank you very much.

I spent at least an hour reading through various blogs and articles outlining how to find out who owned a website when they had paid for anonymity. There was a whole bunch of useless junk seemingly for a lot of people who didn't know what they were doing. But hey, it was the Internet, so that was normal.

Disappointment started to creep into each keystroke I pressed until finally, I had the breakthrough I was looking for. A blog post from TechStar wrote that if I could find out the website's IP address, I could use another search to find out what other domains that IP address owned. This meant that if the anti-Buthaire website owner had other domains that were public, I could figure out who owned it. I didn't know how likely that would be, because if they protected one site, it seemed likely they would protect any others they owned.

I followed the blog's instructions to do a whole bunch of nerd stuff you probably don't care about and would take too long to explain. It involved command prompts and pinging stuff. Okay, I'll shut up now. Well, about the nerd stuff, anyway. Within minutes, I had the anti-Buthaire website's IP address. Within a few more, I nerded my way toward the promise land. I held my breath and closed my eyes as I hit enter, hoping there would be other websites listed at that IP address.

I opened my eyes slowly and couldn't believe what I saw. I hit the lottery. I rubbed my eyes and checked the screen again. I wouldn't have to do a WhoIs search on the website listed to see if the owner was public. It was quite clear who the owner was. I thrust my arms in the air and yelled, "I just won the Internet!" I thought about getting up and dancing, but I remembered my high-fiving incident with Ben and decided against it.

Guess what the name of the website was? It was Randy-warblemachersuperstar.com. Boom! If ever there was a time for a mic drop, it was then. True, I hadn't rapped anything, but this was big. I scanned the website's contents. It outlined his sports and drama career highlights. I noticed that these highlights didn't seem to show his role as the wounded dog I discovered during our musical, Santukkah! Surprising.

I was ecstatic. Energy surged through my body like never before. Randy Warblemacher was going down like the Halloween Dance! If you haven't heard that story, I'll tell it to you sometime. I couldn't help myself and did a whole lot of dabbing in celebration and nearly knocked myself out, but it was worth it. When nerds celebrate, you always run the risk that bad things can happen. Sometimes, you can't let that stop you.

For the first time in a long time, I couldn't wait to get to school. The next day was going to be a great day.

11

The next morning, I sat in advisory, whispering my findings to Just Charles. I swore him, Ben, and Sammie to secrecy. We had to plan a big reveal to take down Randy. I worried that it would make him even more popular with the students and even some teachers, but the idea of Principal Buthaire unleashing his lunacy on Randy and perhaps even taking some focus off of me, made me giddy. I thought it was totally worth it.

My story was interrupted as Mr. Gifford entered the room and called out to Mrs. Callahan, "Can I have Austin for the rest of Advisory?"

Mrs. Callahan furrowed her brow, but said, "Sure."

I stood up and shrugged at Just Charles. "It has to be better than getting called down to Butt Hair's," I whispered.

I walked over to Mr. Gifford. He didn't look happy. Maybe I spoke too soon about the day being a great one.

"Good morning, Austin," he said, with pity in his eyes.

"Good morning. What's going on, sir?" I asked, cautiously.

I followed Mr. Gifford out of the classroom and into the hallway. Ben, Cheryl Van Snoogle-Something, and Zack Kempler were all waiting for us in the hallway. None of them looked happy.

I looked at Ben. He shrugged. "He didn't tell us anything," he whispered.

Mr. Gifford looked at us as we walked. "There's some bad news I need to tell you about. Looks like a volcano experiment accidentally exploded, setting off a chain reaction that plastered Zack's presentation board with lava and knocked over Cheryl Van Snoogle-Something's Leaning Tower of Pisa engineering demonstration, which smashed Austin and Ben's robot hand."

"Are you kidding me?" I yelled. I took a deep breath, trying to soothe my anger. Stupid volcano. I mean, who thought they would really win with an exploding volcano! It's been done a thousand times.

"I don't believe this!" Ben yelled.

"Whose volcano was it?" I asked, fuming.

Mr. Gifford shrugged. "That's the funny thing about it. There's no presentation board and nobody was actually assigned that space. Must've been a paperwork error. We'll see who shows up later to claim it."

"Is this Butt Hair's doing?" I asked Ben.

He shrugged. I looked over at Cheryl Van Snoogle-Something. Tears filled her eyes. Zack actually looked relieved. I wondered if his was the project that explored why old people smelled. I wouldn't want to give that presentation, either. Especially to a bunch of old, and most likely, smelly judges.

As we walked into the gym, Mr. Gifford headed straight for our remote project display area. The gym was empty except for Mr. Muscalini, who was waiting for us, pacing. I ignored him as I rushed straight to my robot, Ben at my heels. It was bad.

Our robot's exoskeleton, the main piece we made on the 3D printer, was cracked in half. Wires were melted. Lava had dried on the camera lens. I didn't even want to look inside to see the state of the microchip or the microphone.

Mr. Gifford walked up next to Ben and me, rubbing his beard. He tried to sound optimistic, "It could probably, maybe, with a little luck-"

Mr. Muscalini stepped forward and pushed Mr. Gifford to the side. "Step aside, Gifford. This is my gym. My territory. Gather 'round, team." He waved us all in.

Mr. Muscalini stood in front of Ben, Cheryl Van Snoogle-Something, Zack and me. He exhaled quickly and flexed, psyching himself up. I was not in the mood for another pep talk. After a minute, he finally spoke, "Yes, your backs are against the wall. The battle has been lost. But the war ain't over."

I looked at Cheryl Van Snoogle-Something. She looked like she was going to cry again. I was borderline. Mr.

Muscalini continued, "When life knocks you down and you fall on your face, what do you do, Ms. Van Snoogle-Something?"

Cheryl Van Snoogle-Something fought back tears and shrugged.

"How about you, Gordo?" Mr. Muscalini asked.

"Get up?"

"No!" Mr. Muscalini yelled. "You turn it into a burpee!"

"What the heck is a burpee?" Zack asked.

I shrugged. Ben shook his head. Cheryl Van Snoogle-Something cried.

Mr. Muscalini's face contorted like he was trying to bench press a thousand pounds with his pinkies.

"Let me try to put it in nerd words." He thought for a moment and continued, "Okay, I got it," Mr. Muscalini said, holding his fist up for a bump from Mr. Gifford. Mr. Gifford high fived it awkwardly. Mr. Muscalini shook his head and continued, "I don't speak nerd, but I'll give it a try." He took a deep breath, "It's not the number of breaths we take, but the number of moments that take our breath away." He turned away from us and shook his head. "No, that's not it." He turned back and said, "You have to look through the rain to see the rainbow." Mr. Muscalini looked up at the ceiling. "What is wrong with me? I need protein!" He stormed off, stomping his feet and muttering to himself.

Mr. Gifford scratched his head and stepped in front of us. "There's still time to fix it." He didn't look all that confident.

"Can't you postpone the science fair?" I asked.

"Sadly, we cannot. We have news crews and judges coming."

"This really isn't fair," Ben said. "We all worked really hard on these. Why shouldn't we be allowed to participate?"

"It's just an unfortunate accident. I'm sorry, there's nothing we can do. You have time to fix it and you can still present your projects-" He looked at our poor robot hand and continued, "in whatever states they're in. I can give you passes to miss first period and regroup here."

Zack said, "I'm good. I'll just head back to class."

Mr. Gifford shrugged and said, "Okay. What about the rest of you?"

As disappointed as I was, I knew I had to at least try to fix our project. Randy wouldn't let me out of the bet.

After Cheryl Van Snoogle-Something walked over to her table, I leaned into Ben and whispered, "Do you think Randy could've sabotaged us?"

Ben tapped his chin as he thought. "It's very possible. I mean, how does a volcano just go off? Don't you have to add chemicals to it?"

I nodded. "Yep. Unless there was some sort of compartment separating the ingredients that somehow broke, someone would've had to add baking soda and vinegar together to make the volcano erupt."

"Seems unlikely," Ben added.

"And nobody knows whose project it is? That seems really suspicious."

"You think Randy would go through all the trouble of building a second project just to beat you?" Ben asked.

"Yes, but I have no idea how to prove it," I said, scratching my head. "But I'm going to. We got him on the website. Now we're going to get him on this."

"How are we going to do that?"

"Did Mr. Gifford say something about a news crew?"

Ben smiled. "I believe he did."

"What if the website bandit was outed on the news?"

BEN and I tried to work out a plan to turn Randy in live on the news, but I wasn't sure how to get on camera. And I still wanted to get Randy for sabotaging our project. I wished I had a secret spy camera or microphone. I wanted to hear what he was saying. I knew he was too arrogant to keep it entirely to himself. He obviously hadn't told Sophie, but I knew how often Derek blabbed to his teammates. I figured Randy did the same.

So when I saw Randy heading toward the locker room with David Betz, I knew I had to follow them. I did what I learned from watching detective shows with my dad. I kept an eye on them from a distance, giving them at least fifty feet and a few clusters of people in between to avoid detection.

Randy entered the locker room behind David Betz. I was hoping to get there before the door shut completely so as to slip in quietly. I hopped into a run as soon as they disappeared from sight, but was interrupted by Mr. Muscalini.

"I didn't know you knew how to run, Davenport. That was what you were trying to do, right?"

I slowed to a stop and turned to him. "Umm, yes. Is that all?" I looked at the closed locker room door.

"Hey, you're a science geek, right Davenport?"

"I guess so," I said, watching Randy disappear into the locker room.

"Do you think I could add Chizpurfle fang to my smoothies?"

"Umm, isn't that from Harry Potter?"

"Yeah. I've been reading it with my lady friend. She's all into words and stuff."

"I'm sorry, but there's no such thing."

"You sure?"

"Pretty sure," I said.

"It's not on one of those science thingies, the periodic bench?"

"Periodic table?"

"Yeah, that," Mr. Muscalini said, pointing at me. "I was close. It's still periodic furniture."

"Yes, very close, but unfortunately it doesn't exist in the Muggle world."

"Aww, man. But it's supposed to counteract the Draught of the Living Death. I figured that would have anti-aging characteristics." He rubbed the outer corners of his eyes. "I'm getting crow's feet. I hate being a Muggle."

"Join the club, sir." Cherry Avenue ain't no Hogwarts. "I gotta go. I'll see you later."

"Godspeed, Davenport."

I entered the locker room quietly. All gym classes and most team activities had been cancelled because of the science fair, so it was likely to be nearly empty. I didn't want Randy to know I was there.

I heard footsteps coming toward me. I didn't have time to exit the locker room, so I opened the closest door, jumped in, and pulled it shut. It was not my best decision. It was dark and loud. The ground beneath me rumbled. I didn't read the sign on the door, if there even was one, so I wasn't certain where I was, but it seemed to be some sort of utility room.

The footsteps passed by. Randy said, "Oh, man. If you could've seen the look on Davenfart's face when he realized we copied his project..."

Anger surged through my body with such force, I thought that Randy might be able to hear my heart pounding through the door. I fought with myself to keep quiet. I won. But then I realized I also lost.

I turned the knob on the door, but it was stuck. I jiggled the handle. Nothing. I pushed on the door. It didn't budge. Uh, oh. I was locked in the utility room and now there was nobody in the locker room to help me. I reached into my pocket and pulled out my phone. I flipped the flashlight app on, so I could at least see what was going on. It was something I regret to this day.

Zorch and I were going to have words. I ran my phone across the room, scanning a few feet at a time. It was a disgusting mess. I wondered if anyone had been in here, like ever. Spider webs, dust, and other debris covered virtually every inch of the room. It wasn't that big. I could see past a few different mechanical units, all humming and seemingly barely holding together at the seams. There was a concrete wall on the far side and some sort of crawl space. I wasn't sure where it went and I didn't plan on finding out.

With Phys Ed class and team activities canceled for the science fair, banging on the door was likely a losing endeavor. Instead, I dialed Ben on my phone. I had one bar. Wait. Zero bars. No, one bar if I held the phone above my head while balancing on my tippy toes. I waited for it to connect, but it never did. I was very disappointed in my carrier. Who didn't offer coverage in ancient school utility rooms encased in concrete?

I texted Ben an S.O.S. message. I hit send, but, of course, it failed to deliver. Ugh. I could wait it out and hope that someone realized I was missing and that Mr. Muscalini remembered I went to the locker room after our Hogwarts potion conversation, which was a 0.1% chance, or I could see where the crawl space went.

I chose the 0.1% chance. I had faith in Mr. Muscalini. Well, not really, but I kept telling myself that because I didn't want to go through the crawl space. After a good twenty minutes, I decided to at least take a look in the crawl space.

I took a deep breath and walked slowly toward it. My phone lit the way with one hand and I used my other to swat the seemingly infinite number of cobwebs. I turned to my right to head around a rumbling machine and found myself face to face with a spider that looked more like a gigantic octopus. I could see its knee caps and biceps. I mean, this thing must've worked out with Mr. Muscalini and hit the protein shakes.

I shrieked like a two-year old, punched the spider in the face, and hopped back, falling into the machine. "Ouch!" I yelled, more angry than hurt. Well, I was emotionally scarred, but physically, there was little damage. The spider was unfazed.

Once I realized it was only a whale-sized spider that could eat me with one bite staring back at me, I sidestepped away from it. I heard the tearing of fabric and then felt a pull on my leg. I stopped moving and looked down at my jeans.

"Oh, great." There was a huge rip right under my back pocket and around the side of my thigh, stopping right under my front pocket. My red and white polka dotted boxers stuck out from the hole. I couldn't wait for the entire to school to see me in my underwear. It happened once already that year. I was not looking forward to another show. My guess was that I was going to get detention for showing the school my underwear.

I kept navigating the utility room as carefully as possible. When I reached the crawl space, I squatted down and ducked my head toward the ground. My phone lit a good ways down the mini tunnel. It was dirty, but I was small enough to fit. I just didn't know where it went. It might not go anywhere and then I would have to back out of the tunnel, which I thought would be a bit more difficult.

After a few minutes of thought, I didn't have any better ideas, so I decided to head into the abyss before me. I lay down on my stomach, the phone lighting my way. I pulled my shirt up over my mouth and entered the uncertainty. Did death await? Maybe. What about more pant ripping? Probably.

12

I slithered through the crawl space like a snake. Or at least that's what I was going for. It's really hard. You try it sometime. I mean, I don't know how snakes do it. I even used my arms and I could barely make it through. And it was disgusting. The dust and filth were like nothing I had ever seen. Or tasted. The good news was that if dust had calories, I wouldn't need to eat for about a week.

I came to a crossroads in the crawl space. I could continue forward or turn right. I stopped for a minute to rest and think. I shined my flashlight app down each tunnel. The path straight ahead seemed longer, but I could hear machinery, so I figured there would at least be a potential exit. It might be locked, but it was at least possible I could survive by going in that direction.

To the left, I couldn't see much of anything, but if I listened carefully, I could hear voices, and even pick up some sentences, depending on who was talking and how loud.

I wasn't sure who it was, but I heard a somewhat familiar voice say, "I noticed there were two interesting robotics projects. It's such a blossoming area in the scientific field these days. I'd like to speak with both of them to see where their interests lie and how they approached their projects."

Principal Buthaire paused and then said, "Yes. Yes, indeed. I can certainly introduce you to Randy Warblemacher and his partner. The other student unfortunately had serious technical difficulties with his project, so I wouldn't recommend it. I don't think it's ready for the limelight just yet."

"Typical," I said. I was angry. I was face deep in filth, not sure if I would die here and never be found, and Principal Buthaire was attempting to thwart my efforts to destroy Randy on live TV. What a turd.

"Still, we'd like to speak to him broadly about the field. We don't have to talk about the project."

"I'd be glad to!" I yelled. And then, "Prince Butt Hair, I hate you!"

I decided to follow the voices. I wasn't sure how they were getting to me. I guessed it was a vent, but I wasn't sure. I bent myself around the corner and continued toward the voices. As I got closer, I could see light seeping through slits in a vent.

Energized, I continued toward the light, army crawling. My forearms burned. My leg was scraped and probably bloody from my ripped jeans, and I was coated with twelve layers of dirt. If I got out of there, the girls would go crazy. Sophie would dump Randy on the spot and beg for my forgiveness. Muahahaha! My plan was working...

As I got to the end of the tunnel, I reached forward and tried to push the vent open. It didn't budge. I scooted up closer and dug my feet into the sides of the crawl space. I pushed with all my might. I let out an epic battle cry and a tiny squeaker of a fart. I forced the vent open. I must have ripped the screws out of the wall. It swung open like a door and then clanked against the wall on the outside. I looked out to see a blast of light and a whole bunch of confused faces.

I slithered out and stood up. I shielded my eyes from the light. At first, there was a hush from those around, but then the chatter quickly rose back up even stronger than before. I looked around. Nearly the half the school was staring at me.

I looked down and straightened my disgustingly dirty and torn jeans. One pant leg was completely disconnected from the rest of my jeans. I ran my fingers through my hair and then shook it out like a shampoo commercial. Chunks of dirt, dust, and pebbles pelted the floor. I was waiting for all the girls to line up and ask me out. All I got was a bunch of old ladies gasping. Well, Mrs. Truglio, one of our librarians, nearly fainted, too. I like to think it was because of my new stylish look.

Without warning, Calvin Conklin, a semi-famous local news anchor from Channel 2 stepped forward, thrusting a microphone in my face. It was his familiar voice that I had heard earlier.

He saddled up next to me and stared at the camera.

"Calvin Conklin here in the field at Cherry Avenue Middle School. We are in the midst of some..." he looked me up and down and then continued, "some strange stuff going on." Calvin turned to me and said, "What happened? Where did you come from? Are you from this dimension?"

I was confused and didn't know what to say. I think I may have been delirious. "I was just down in the mines."

"The mines? What do you mean? Are you from the past?" Calvin looked back at the camera. "Calvin Conklin here with breaking news. We're live with, perhaps, the first time traveler ever captured on film."

I heard one of Randy's buddies say, "Nice pants." The crowd laughed.

"It's the new rage," I said. "Why wear two pant legs when you can wear just one? It's huge in Europe."

I was about to reveal Randy's dark secret to the world, but I was distracted by a primal scream and stomping feet. Before I knew what was going on, people were flying everywhere. And then Amanda Gluskin surged from the crowd, revenge in her eyes. Apparently, she found out that Derek wasn't into her. Or this was her way of showing me her affection.

Despite my cat-like reflexes (think Garfield), I wasn't quick enough to evade her attack. She grabbed my shoulders, spun me around, and swept my feet out from under me with a swift kick. I crumpled to the ground. The crowd froze. I really appreciated their support.

At least they were better than Calvin Conklin. He turned into a WWE announcer. "Oh, she's taken the time traveler down! She dropped him like a toilet seat! She's taking him for a ride on the pain train!"

I struggled for my life, as Amanda sat on my back, clasped her hands beneath my chin, and pulled up as if she was trying to break me in half, which I'm pretty sure she was. She had me in a full Camel Clutch and there was nothing I could do.

Well, except let out a whelp that I am told started off sounding like a bleating goat and ended like a dying goat farting into a megaphone. If you've never heard what that sounds like, I am also told that you don't ever want to know what that sounds like. And then the air stopped traveling to my brain and everything went black.

13

I woke up in the nurse's office and somehow, it was determined that I was good to go. I was breathing normally and that was all they needed to see. They didn't seem to care that the idea of Sophie and Randy dating was something that my mind, as brilliant as it was, couldn't seem to compute. My heart was still broken while my ego was shattered. There's nothing like getting beaten up by a girl in middle school, which just happens to get caught by a news crew.

On the plus side, it got a million views on YouTube and I got to wear a cool pair of sweat pants from the lost and found. Carbon dating suggested they were from 1976. The fashion police (the cheerleading squad) suggested I should never wear them again. They didn't actually tell me that. Their pointing and laughing made it pretty clear, though.

The rumors swirled. Within no time, the story was that the zoo had to sedate Amanda with elephant tranquilizers just to get her off me, but that may have actually happened. I refused to watch the YouTube videos to know for sure, even though Derek plays it every morning as his daily motivation.

Back to Randy. He and I were going to have words. And not the polite kind. There would be accusations, biting comments, insults, and possibly sarcasm. You know, so a normal day in middle school, minus the Camel Clutch. I wasn't brave enough to try that on him. If I did, it was likely that I would be the first middle schooler ever to be placed in the Camel Clutch twice.

I stood in the hallway outside the nurse's office. Mr. Gifford and Mr. Muscalini stood in front of me.

Mr. Gifford put his hand on my shoulder. "You don't have to do this. I mean, your project, is already, kind of...you know."

"I have to, but...I don't know how to say this. I need you."

"What do you need?" Mr. Gifford said, straightening up.

Mr. Muscalini stepped forward and gently removed Mr. Gifford's hand from my shoulder. "He's talking to me, Geoffrey."

Mr. Gifford looked at me, puzzled. I just nodded.

"Okay," he said, seemingly not sure what the heck was going on. "I'm here if you need me."

"I've got this," Mr. Muscalini said.

We watched Mr. Gifford walk away for a moment before Mr. Muscalini took a deep breath and said, "There is a time when a boy becomes a man. For some, it's their bar mitzvah. For others, when their mustache grows in." He leaned in to inspect my non-existent mustache and shrugged.

"For me, it was when Wendy Cahill kissed me on the playground in fourth grade."

"That was when you knew you became a man?"

"I had chest hair when I joined the Cub Scouts, Davenport. Some of us develop faster than others."

I raised an eyebrow. He was losing me.

"Your moment was definitely not any that I've ever seen, certainly not your wrestling match with Amanda Gluskin."

"That wasn't a match. She attacked me." I felt that was an important distinction to make.

"But your moment is coming. I think your moment is now. Are you ready to seize it?" He looked at me expectantly.

"Yes!" I yelled.

"What are you ready to do?"

"I'm ready to take down Randy Warblemacher!" I yelled, feeling more alive than I had ever felt.

"Wait, you're taking down Warblemacher? He's my star player! I thought you were talking about that psycho Gluskin!"

"Sorry, sir. Not my fault." I stepped past him. "Now, if you'll excuse me, I have business to attend to." No, I wasn't going to see Max Mulvihill. I was going to have a showdown with Randy Warblemacher on his turf. It was time to become a man.

I entered the gym with one thing in mind. Total domination. It was a unique feeling. I kind of liked it. Normally, I entered the gym with fear seeping from my pores. My eyes scanned the room, searching for Randy. Target acquired. I navigated the busy main passage like a middle schooler on a mission.

I was in Randy's face, well, more like his chest, before he knew what was coming.

"I know you did it, Warblemonster!" I wasn't sure if the new nickname would stick, but I was reasonably pleased with it.

"Did what?" Randy said, taking a step back. "Personal space, dude."

"Ruined my project," I said, simply.

"Oh, I thought you meant stealing your girlfriend."

My blood started to boil. I couldn't find the right words.

Randy continued, "I beat you at everything, Davenfart. I beat you in basketball. I beat you in the school musical. I beat you with Sophie. I even beat you in the last science competition in class. Remember the balloon race? I'm sorry your project got broken. I assure you I didn't do it. I don't need to cheat to beat you."

"I'm going to prove you cheated and you're gonna pay!" I had no idea what he was going to pay with, but it sounded good.

"Settle down, Austin." Mr. Gifford held me by the shoulders and had Ben at his side. "We will look into every avenue. We are taking this very seriously. But until there is evidence, you would be wise to avoid accusing other students." He whispered the rest in my ear, "Especially those on the basketball team."

He made a good point, but in the moment, I wasn't thinking straight.

"Ben, take him outside to cool down."

"Let's go, Austin," Ben said, ushering me away from Randy's booth. "Let's get some air."

Ben led me out of the gym and into the atrium. I was still

amped up and pretty sure I had not become a man in that moment. And what do you know? The first person we saw when we hit the atrium was none other than the heart-breaking, soul-crushing Sophie Rodriquez.

"What's wrong? Are you okay?" Sophie asked, most likely pretending to be concerned, with a cold-hearted look that was still really cute because she scrunched up her nose when she said it.

"I'm fine," I said, defensively. "You wouldn't believe me, anyway," I said, harshly.

"Why not?" She asked, annoyed.

"Because you didn't believe me when I told you Randy was a jerk when I was your boyfriend. Now he's your blah-your blahfriend." I coughed. "Sorry, pesky hair ball."

She didn't say anything. Well, with words. Her face said a lot. And none of it was good. I didn't know if I should talk before she exploded or just run.

I decided to get it all out. "He stole my idea. And he sabotaged my project and a few others."

"He wouldn't do that," Sophie said.

"See? Of course, you believe him over me. I thought YOU were different. If he wasn't so good at everything and looked like a normal kid, nobody would like him. He's rude and arrogant. And a cheater. I can't believe I'm the only one who sees it." I looked Sophie in the eyes and said, "Good luck with him."

14

That night at home, I just wanted to be left alone. I wondered if I should become a monk. That way, nobody would bother me. True, I didn't want to shave my head or wear a strange-looking robe dress, but no career is perfect.

I sat slumped in my bean bag chair, staring at the fabulously boring ceiling, pondering all of the events of my life that had led me to this point. I heard footsteps outside my door and then a grunt. Of course, my dad ignored my 'Do not disturb' sign clearly posted on my door. I heard his voice squeeze through the crack underneath the door. "Hey, bud. I don't have a lot to say, but I would like to talk to you. I can do it like this lying on the floor or we can talk like men, face to face."

I rolled out of my bean bag chair with a huff and slowly climbed to my feet. I walked over to the door and unlocked it. I didn't even bother to open it. I just walked over to my bed and plopped into it, face down. I didn't feel like having a manly, face to face talk. He was going to have to talk to my butt.

The door squeaked when it opened. My dad walked across the room and sat down on the edge of my bed. "There's not much room on this bad boy. You're getting big."

"Why do they call it a twin bed when it only sleeps one person?" I asked.

"Son, I'm a very wise man, but the universe has some mysteries that can't be cracked."

I nodded and rolled over. He was too good of a dad to make him talk to my butt the whole conversation.

"Do you want to talk about everything that's going on?" My dad asked, gently.

"Not particularly. I'd just like to quit," I said, defeated.

"But what about all your hard work? And Ben? Do you want to let him down?"

"All my hard work was wasted. And Ben doesn't care. He's just as upset as I am. We can't win, so who cares?"

"So you shouldn't give something your best because you think you might lose? Doesn't seem like a great philosophy."

"I'm just so sick and tired of Randy. He wins at everything. He will always win at everything. So why should I bother?"

"You're just going to give up on life? Drop out of school? Ride the rails like a hobo?"

"What the heck are you talking about? What's a hobo?"

"It's a long story," my dad said, laughing.

"I was gonna join the circus or maybe become a monk."

"I don't think you would look that great in a robe."

"Yeah, that was one of my main concerns," I said. "What is it, my skinny legs?"

"I think so." My dad got serious again. "There will always be people that are better than you at things. There are seven billion people in the world. You can't worry about it. Be the best Austin you can be. That's all you have control over. Challenge yourself. See how good you can be, regardless of what anyone else does."

"That's the point, dad. I stink. Like a fart. A smelly, smelly fart."

"That's not true. You can't say that stuff about yourself. You're amazing in so many ways. Deep down, you know you're a special kid. They don't make too many like you. I know you don't always fit in, but that's because you're so special."

"Sometimes, I just want to be a normal idiot like the rest of the kids at school, who run without fear of knocking themselves out by punching themselves."

"I know, bud. You only knocked yourself out once. But let's just lay out a plan to fix the project. I know if you get back into it, you'll feel a lot better."

"I don't care," I said.

"If you did care, what would you fix?"

I decided to play along. "Well, we need to fix the cracked exoskeleton and rewire a whole bunch of stuff. It needs a lot of cleaning, too."

"Do what you can. If it doesn't work, it doesn't work. You

could explain the accident, present the concepts, talk about how you can make it stronger, and go through the future of the project. If I were a judge, I would be good with that."

Most of me wanted to roll back over and let my butt answer him, but there was a small part of me that wanted to push forward. I tried to focus on that. Thoughts of giving up pummeled my brain, but I kept combatting them, telling myself not to give up.

"Stand up and let's do this," my dad said with enthusiasm. He sounded a little bit too much like Mr. Muscalini.

I nodded and drew in a big breath and then let it out slow. I pushed myself up off the bed and shook out my arms and legs.

"high-fiving?" my dad asked.

"No, I've retired from high-fiving," I said, remembering my last disaster with Ben. "It's a long story, so let's get going."

15

Ben was over in ten minutes, ready to go. We were in my room, slurping Capri-Suns and strategizing.

Ben looked at me and said, "All you gotta do is beat Randy, take down Butt Hair, and win back Sophie."

I laughed. "Oh, is that it? All this time, I thought it was going to be difficult. I'm sure I can find a YouTube video on how to do all that."

My dad stepped into my doorway and asked, "How's it going?"

I looked down at the hodge podge of parts in front of me and said, "I really don't know. It may be a bust."

"Keep pushing forward. You need anything else?"

"A YouTube video on how to do all this?"

My dad frowned. "That might be a tough one. You're going to have to figure this out on your own."

My dad turned to leave.

"Hey, Dad? I need your advice." I put down the wires and turned toward him in my swivel chair.

"What's that?" My dad stepped back into my room and walked toward me.

"I heard Randy tell someone that he copied my project. Well, he actually said, 'we.' I think he may have also sabotaged my project."

"Okay, so what're you thinking?"

"Well, if I turn him in and somebody actually believes me, Randy will lose and get in trouble, which he deserves. But that means Sophie could get in trouble, and I don't think she was involved. So, I don't want to turn him in."

"I guess you have a choice to make."

"Which one is the right one?"

"They both could be right. Randy deserves to get in trouble. Sophie doesn't. Which one feels more right?"

16

I worked all night after dinner with Ben, attempting to recreate our Magic Mano. That's Spanish for magic hand. I could've used some magic right about then. Robot headquarters was active, but not necessarily making much progress. And morale was low.

My dad peeked his head into my room again. He was helicoptering, I guess to make sure I didn't actually climb out the window and head off for the circus. "What's the plan, gentlemen?"

Ben looked around the room, confused. "He's talking to us," I said.

"Oh, nobody calls me a gentleman. My mother says I'm a caveman."

"I was trying to give you something to live up to," my dad said.

"So, we need to fix the exoskeleton first."

"That's going to be a problem," Ben said.

"Why?" my dad asked.

I answered, "The library is closed for the night and they

don't open up again until 9:30 in the morning, too late to make the piece again."

"Can we glue it?" Ben asked.

"That's pretty much all we can do," I said, rubbing my chin.

"What do you need?" my dad asked.

I thought for a minute. "Pizza."

Ben added, "Lots of it."

"You think the cheese will hold it all together?" my dad asked.

I laughed. "Not sure, but we have glue. We could use meatballs."

"And cash. Fifty bucks each ought to do it."

My dad frowned at Ben.

Ben shrugged. "It was worth a shot.'"

"I'll take care of it," my dad said, and headed out of my room.

I looked at Ben and said, "I don't have enough wiring to get this to reach all the way up to the hand."

"Can we go to the store?" Ben asked.

I looked at the clock. "It's too late. Nothing is open now and nothing will be open before tomorrow's presentation."

"Amazon?"

"Even they're not that quick." We sat there for a few minutes, just staring at the scattered parts. And then I had an idea. "Or..." I said, standing up. "Follow me."

"Uh, oh. What are you gonna do?" Ben asked.

"You'll see."

"Oh, boy."

I walked out of my room, Ben at my heels. We headed down the hallway into the den. My parents were watching TV together, sitting on the couch under a blanket.

"Pizza will be here in thirty minutes," my dad said.

"Uh, huh," I said, not paying attention.

I stopped in front of the entertainment center and opened the cabinet door.

My dad asked, "Austin, what are you doing?"

"Nothing," I said, moving DVDs off of the DVD player. "Hey, Dad?"

"Yeah, bud. What're you doing?" he asked, a little nervous.

"You remember that fifty bucks you were going to give me?"

"That wasn't going to happen."

"Let's pretend it was. I need the DVD player." I unhooked some cables.

"Uhh, okay."

"This has been acting up lately, anyway."

"No, it hasn't. It's worked totally fine," my mother said.

"Don't you remember when it wasn't working a few weeks ago?"

"Yeah, your brother unplugged it."

"Still, it wasn't working," I said. "It's very unreliable." I slipped the DVD player out of the cabinet, held it up to my ear, and shook it. "Sounds broken."

"No, it doesn't," my dad said.

I ignored him. "I'm not convinced this will ever work again. The good news is I can recycle it. I can use it to make my project work and save the earth at the same time. And I need one of your speakers and wires."

"My surround sound?" Dad said, disappointed. "Okay, bud. Have at it."

"Thanks, dad. You're the best!"

"What about me?" My mom asked.

"You're the best, too."

"Thank you, sweetie."

I went back into my room with Ben, the DVD player under my arm. I placed it upside down on my desk.

"The motor should be good to use from here," I said as I pointed to the DVD player. I handed Ben a screwdriver and said, "Take apart that speaker. We just need the wiring."

"Will do, boss."

"I think this might actually work."

"That makes one of us," Ben said.

"Thanks for the support, bro."

"No problem. I'm here to help."

We worked late into the night. Our project was functioning. Mr. Robot looked like it had been through open-heart surgery, but it worked. We were exhausted. Ben ended up sleeping over. It was nearly 4 A.M. when we passed out, less than four hours until school started. It was going to be an interesting day.

17

I woke up a man, or more accurately, a boy on a mission. I got dressed, ate a hearty breakfast of corn flakes with a glass of chocolate milk (a chilled glass and shaken, not stirred, of course), and made my way to school.

My dad dropped Ben and me off before school started so we could get our project set up again. Thankfully, there weren't any new stupid volcanos in our section. I still wanted to know who had ruined everything, but nobody showed up to claim any of the lava. The bus let out at 7:45 A.M. We were done setting up just as the kids started to flow in. I know, bad choice of words. Lava. Flow. Too soon.

I went outside to get a drink of water and then headed back toward the gym, never before so confident to enter the evil place where nerds' dreams of a normal social life die with round balls and sharp words. We had persevered more than we ever had during dodge ball week. Ben, Sammie, and Just Charles were beside me on our way into the science fair alongside half of the sixth-grade class.

Derek stood against the wall, dangling on his crutches,

watching the students as they walked by. I avoided eye contact, but when he saw me and my friends, he called out anyway, "What's up, Davenfart?"

"Really? You're a Davenport, too."

Derek shrugged, "Yeah, but nobody calls me Davenfart. Have fun!" He pumped his fist and said, "Nerds Unite!"

I shook my head and continued on. My first stop was Randy's booth. There was no way in the world I would miss Randy's and Sophie's presentation. It was the first presentation of the day. Apparently, the rest of the school thought the same thing. A crowd had gathered around their booth, mainly sixth and seventh grade girls wanting to get a closer look at Randy, the Science Dweeb. I'm glad my mom taught me that word. It was very fitting every time I spoke about Randy.

I inched up toward the front, but on the outer rim of the crowd. Ben and Just Charles were right behind me. A judge in a crisp, white, but unnecessary lab coat, stepped forward, and said, "Let us begin. You have three minutes."

Randy smiled, his teeth sparkling for the crowd. "Welcome, science lovers, robot admirers, or just admirers." Randy winked at the front row of girls. Most of them giggled.

I looked at Ben and shook my head and then back at the presentation. Sophie was standing next to Randy, twiddling her thumbs at her waist. I could tell she was nervous. Next to her was something covered under a white sheet. I knew it was their stupid robot that they ripped off from me.

Randy continued his speech, "The field of robotics is growing exponentially. The applications are virtually limitless. When my nana got sick, before she...passed on-" Randy paused and wiped a tear from his eye. The crowd gasped with sympathy, but I knew he was acting. Randy was the star from our musical. He was a gifted fake cryer, even though he cheated in our crying contest. It's a long story.

"Sorry," Randy continued, "She needed help, but didn't want it. We tried to get her to move in with us. I gladly would've given my room to her. We tried to get her to accept a home health aide, but she wanted to remain independent. It is because of my nana that I designed, 'Homie', a home-help robot." He looked over at Sophie and the robot, and shot air guns at it.

Sophie pulled the sheet from Homie, the dumb robot, with dramatic flair. The crowd oohed and aahed. It was pretty meh as far as I was concerned. Except for Sophie. She was still amazing. As angry as I was at her, I still wished I was her boyfriend.

Sophie stepped forward. "We designed Homie to respond to voice commands in case its owner had difficulty with motor functioning or perhaps was even paralyzed. We'll demonstrate it now."

Randy moved Homie to a long table. He looked at the crowd, "It's light and very compact."

Sophie placed a water bottle at the other end. Homie faced away from the water bottle. Sophie cleared her throat and said, "Homie, please turn to your right, 180 degrees." Homie turned around to face the water bottle.

"Homie, please move forward." Homie rolled forward, its motor revving. As it approached the water bottle, Sophie said, "Stop." Homie stopped. The crowd cheered and chattered.

Sophie smiled at the crowd and then continued to give commands to Homie.

As cute as Sophie was, my eyes were pulled somewhere else. I looked off to the side of the presentation and noticed something rather strange. Through the crowd I could see

Kevin Minor, one of Randy's and Derek's teammates, sitting with his back to the presentation. He was the only person in the area not watching. I looked over at Ben and nodded in Kevin's direction. He frowned and then shrugged. He was super helpful.

I found it odd, so I slid out from the few people gathered around me to get a better angle and look. He leaned over the table in front of him, seemingly staring at an empty tablecloth. His hands were underneath the table as if he were trying to hide them. I scooted around a few booths and circled back, trying to avoid detection.

When I got close enough, I bent down and pretended to tie my shoe behind an empty table. I stayed down there hoping that if Kevin saw me, he'd forget I was there eventually. I know, it was really cutting-edge ninja stuff. After a minute, I began crawling underneath the table next to Kevin, the tablecloth concealing my stealth maneuver. I made it to the table's closest edge to him. I lifted the table cloth a smidge and peeked underneath it. I couldn't see Kevin, so I figured he couldn't see me. I reached across to his table and lifted up his table cloth.

What I saw was truly amazing and gratifying. Every time

Sophie gave a command, Kevin followed with the same command on a hand-held controller. They were cheating! I felt like Toto, the dog from The Wizard of Oz, when he revealed the man behind the curtain. The all-powerful Randy was going down. I pumped my fist and nearly yanked the table cloth from the table like a magician, although by accident.

I heard Kevin say, "What the-"

I dropped the table cloth and remained as still as possible. I didn't know how long to wait before heading back out to the crowd. I took a peek out of the side of the table and the coast seemed clear. I rolled out and scrambled to my knees. I looked around as I pretended to tie my shoe again, er, I mean, I implemented evasive ninjitsu maneuvers.

My chest was pounding. But nobody seemed to care where I was. All I heard was clapping and lots of chatter about how awesome the project was. It was so unfair! I was about to yell out, "Cheater!" but then I looked at Sophie and I couldn't do it. As mad as I was at the whole situation, I wasn't convinced she was in on the whole thing. I couldn't imagine her cheating to win. Randy, on the other hand, that was his style.

I stood there seething. The rest of the crowd was cheering like Randy and Sophie just won the Super Bowl. I heard Sophie say to Randy, "Wow! You really came through. When you didn't let me test it with you before the presentation, I thought we were going to be in trouble, but it worked perfectly!"

Randy gave her a hug. My stomach churned. A number of people surrounded the two of them, cheering and patting them on the back. A few girls joined the hug, most likely just to get some Randy time.

I didn't know how to handle the cheating. Based on what

Sophie had just said, I was pretty certain that she had nothing to do with it, and even though she and I hadn't been getting along all that well, or at all, I still didn't want to get her in trouble. I was glad I didn't accuse them then and there. I needed some time to calm down and figure things out.

Ben walked over to me and whispered, "What'd you find out?"

"The whole thing is a sham." I looked over to see Randy beaming at me, his smug face asking for a Kung-Fu kick. Unfortunately, my Kung-Fu skills were rusty. And by rusty, I mean nonexistent. Ninja, yes. Kung Fu, no.

"What do you mean?"

"It's not voice activated. Kevin Minor was operating it with a hand-held controller."

"What?" he yelled, a little too loud.

"Shhh," I said. "Yeah, it's bad, but Sophie doesn't know anything about it."

"How do you know?"

"I just know. The tough part is going to be telling her without her thinking I'm attacking Randy, which of course, I am, and will enjoy more than life itself. I'm gonna hang here until the crowd dies down and then try to talk to her."

"Ok. Adiós, muchacho."

"See ya," I said with a nod.

After a few minutes of me pretending to tie my shoes, the crowd was all but gone. I waited until Randy walked away from the table, seemingly headed out of the gym.

I walked up to Sophie's booth. "Hey," I said, quietly.

"Hey," Sophie said.

"You're a great presenter," I said.

"Thanks," she said, her cheeks reddening. "I thought you hated me."

"Only on Wednesdays."

"It is Wednesday."

I shrugged. "That's too bad. If it makes you feel any better, I like you a lot all the other days." I could feel my face rapidly morphing into a pinkish hue.

Sophie smiled. "It does. I just wish it wasn't Wednesday."

"I'll tell you a secret. I don't really hate you on Wednesdays. Unless you eat the tuna melt in the cafeteria. But that's not my fault. If you eat that, you're just asking for it."

Sophie laughed. "Jerk."

I shrugged. "Sorry. Now that your presentation is over and my robot is a mess of spit, glue, and duct tape, obviously no competition to yours, can you give me a private demonstration?" I asked.

Sophie said, "Sure," and walked over to the robot. She fiddled with it and then flipped the switch on and said, "Homie, please move forward."

Homie didn't move. She repeated her command. Again, nothing. "Homie, reach up." Nothing. "Homie, back up." Nothing. Sophie scratched her head. I could tell she was truly surprised and confused.

I stepped forward. "Is it okay if I take a quick look at it?"

"Sure," Sophie said with a shrug.

"Can I take off the back panel?"

"That's fine."

I unhooked the panel and looked inside of the robot. My suspicions were immediately confirmed. "Hmm," I said, pretending to be confused.

"What's the matter?" Sophie asked.

"Are you sure this is voice activated?"

"Yes, why?" Sophie asked, confused.

"Well, I don't think this is. I saw Kevin Minor earlier with a remote-control handset during your presentation. I didn't really think about it at the time, but if you look inside here, you'll see a receiver in there." I pointed to a black, plastic box. Under black spray paint, I could see the words, '5-channel receiver.' A receiver is what captures the signal from the hand-held controller.

"Oh, my God."

"I'm sorry," I said. I wasn't sorry for telling her. Randy deserved it. But I felt bad because she didn't know.

"I need to find Randy," Sophie said, icily. She stormed off, heading for the gym exit.

I followed her at a distance. I wanted to see Randy finally get what was coming to him. I slipped through the crowd and saw Sophie walk up to him. Well, it was more like stomping, which is understandable.

I stood behind the dogwood tree in the atrium. Sophie and Randy were only a few feet on the other side. I figured they might be able to see me through it, so I sat on a bench with my back to them, a perfect location to maintain my stealthiness, but also hear the conversation.

Sophie went straight for it. "Tell Kevin Minor thanks for helping us in our presentation."

Randy said, "Huh? What? I don't know what you're talking about."

"I know that you cheated. What were you hiding in your backpack that day? I know it wasn't your mother's birthday present."

"It was...it was a gift for you. I couldn't tell you or I would've given it away."

"You're such a liar. I don't think the robot works at all. I don't think it ever did. You cheated. Kevin controlled it behind us. That's why you never let me see it work. That's why you yelled at me when I was about to go into your bag."

That's the last I heard of their conversation, because I was interrupted by a familiar voice, "Hello, Austin."

I looked over to see Randy's mother. Ugh. We had met a few times before, most important and unfortunate, was when my mom thought it would be a good idea to invite the Warblemachers over for Thanksgiving dinner.

I forced a smile. "Hi, Mrs. Warblemacher." I stood up and started to walk away, but she grabbed my arm gently.

"Wasn't that such a great presentation?" She gushed.

"Spectacular," I lied.

"I just admire my Randy so much. I mean, how many other students wanted to do two science projects?"

Oh, really. "What was his second project? I didn't see that one."

"The science fair staple, the volcano. Every science fair needs one, don't you think?"

"Most definitely," I said, bursting into a smile. "I have to run, but it was an absolute pleasure seeing you, Mrs. Warblemacher." It was the only time we'd met that I'd felt that way.

"And if you're looking for Randy, he's right over there." I pointed to Randy and Sophie through the tree.

I circled around the atrium and walked up behind Sophie as I watched Randy walk away with his mother. She turned to me, a tear in her eye.

"You were right. He cheated. I'm sorry I didn't believe you."

I nodded. "It's okay. It hurts to say it, but Randy is a good actor."

"He's a great actor."

I held my hands up. "Let's not get crazy here."

Sophie snorted, as I caught her by surprise. "I just can't

believe he would do that and lie to me," she said, serious again.

I didn't know what to say. I didn't just believe it. I knew it. He was a first-class jerk. And she didn't even know that he had also created a second science fair project designed to explode on his competition, me.

"It gets worse."

"It can't."

"I just saw Mrs. Warblemacher and she told me how proud she was that Randy entered two science fair projects." I studied her face, waiting for a response.

"Two projects?" Sophie asked. She thought about it for a moment. "Oh, Austin, I'm so sorry. It was the volcano, wasn't it?"

I nodded. "That wasn't your fault."

Sophie put her hands on her hips and said, "I don't know what to do."

"Don't do anything," I said.

Sophie looked at me concerned. "What are you going to do? You're going to turn him in, aren't you?

"I thought about it. But no."

"Why not?" Sophie asked, confused.

"Because I can't guarantee that nothing bad will happen to you."

"You would let Randy win to protect me?"

I looked down at my shoes. Suddenly, they seemed very interesting. "Every time."

"Even with everything that happened between us?"

"Yeah, you're right. I changed my mind. I'm turning you both in," I said, trying not to laugh.

Sophie's mouth dropped open. I burst out laughing. She pushed me, playfully. "Jerk. I thought you were serious."

"Okay, I'll be serious. I would always choose what's good

for you over what's bad for Randy. I don't care about him. I care about you." I could feel my face start to burn. I was afraid my face looked like a giant, red balloon.

My watch beeped. I looked down at it and shut off the timer.

"What's that?' Sophie asked.

"It's time for my funeral."

"Huh?"

"Presentation time," I said.

"Oh, I want to see it."

"Please don't. That'll just make it harder."

"Why? I want to support you."

"You're the last person I want to look stupid in front of. I still...you know...well..." I couldn't tell her I still liked her. "I've got to run. I'll see you tomorrow." I turned on my heels and got the heck out of there before I embarrassed myself even more.

I headed back to our remote presentation location. I stopped twice to use the bathroom and have lunch, that's how long it took to get there. I heard Max Mulvihill was offering a shuttle service, but I decided to walk the entire way. When I walked up to the table, Ben was stiff as a board.

I looked at him and said, "All ready?"

He barely nodded, having lost all control of his muscles.

"What's the matter? You're not even speaking in the presentation."

I may have told you this already, but when Ben tried out for the school play, he could barely walk onto the stage due to the fear. He shuffled out in front of Mrs. Funderbunk like a penguin.

Ben moved his arm slowly, eventually pointing toward our robot hand. It was cracked in half again. The part we were forced to glue back in place, didn't hold.

I looked up at the gym ceiling and said, "Why? Why does this always happen to me?"

People started to gather around my booth in anticipation of my presentation, so I figured it was a good idea to stop talking to myself. I walked over to our robot, my soul crushed like a junked car. There was no fixing it. We didn't have glue. We didn't even have mozzarella cheese. And we were out of time.

Not only did we have no time to fix our project, but I also had to present what was left of it entirely by myself. Ben would be no help in that department. Under pressure, he froze. Like literally froze like Han Solo in Carbonite.

For whatever reason, my dad's advice popped into my mind. 'Own it. Do your best and whatever happens, happens.' And then I looked up and saw that it was actually my dad there, speaking. My mom stood beside him, smiling. She gave me a thumbs up. I shrugged. I was happy they were there to support me, but I was still gonna bomb.

I tried to psych myself up and then I saw Sophie step forward toward the front of the crowd. Really? I told her not to come. I looked at her and shook my head.

She mouthed, "Good luck."

I mouthed, "My robot doesn't work. I'm going to bomb."

And then I noticed a small, white canister on our presentation table, next to our robot. There was a tiny card attached with my name on it. I raised an eyebrow as I looked at it. I shrugged and twisted off the top. I immediately regretted it. My face was pummeled with a blast of glitter.

18

A crowd surrounded me as I wiped my eyes and spit out glitter. If you've never eaten glitter, I don't recommend it. Glitter looks a lot better than it tastes.

Ben flipped the card over and read aloud, "From, Amanda Gluskin." He looked at me and said, "You probably should've read that before opening it."

"Thanks for the tip," I said, as if I was not at all thankful for the tip.

"Let's go wash it off," my mother said.

"No!" I said.

Mrs. Funderbunk, our music teacher and the director of our musical, Santukkah!, stepped forward, nodding her head approvingly.

"The show must go on," I said. It was already a disaster. I could at least get points for persistence. A few people cheered. "I got this," I said. It was Go Time. I had glitter all over my face. I looked more like a robot than our real robot.

I knew I didn't have to worry about Ben moving during the presentation. The problem was that when he got nervous, he could still partially move his mouth. And when he gets nervous, his mouth says stupid stuff. So, we had previously both agreed he would focus all of his brain power on finding a happy place somewhere, anywhere that wasn't giving a presentation on a broken science project.

I stepped forward, the crowd shielding their eyes from the light reflecting off of my glittered face. "Welcome," I said, my voice shaking a bit. I looked at Sophie in the crowd. She gave me a thumbs up and a smile. I took a deep breath. "Ben and I built a robot designed to help people in need. I came up with the idea when my idiot, er, older brother broke his foot and needed someone to spoon feed him every meal." The crowd laughed. I was starting to feel a bit better.

"We created a helping hand, if you will, made out of recycled electronic parts and some custom 3D printed parts we designed and made at the local library. It was designed to be voice activated for those who didn't have any or limited control of their hands or arms."

I looked at the sheet by the mess of a robot and then at Mr. Gifford. He nodded at me with a smile. I continued, "Unfortunately, there was an accident. Yesterday, someone's volcano exploded and ruined a few of the projects in our area, ours included."

I took off the sheet to show a robot cracked in half with wires spewing everywhere. The crowd gasped. I looked back at the crowd and said, "Handsome is not so handsome anymore." A few people chuckled.

"I do think we can at least demonstrate how the voice activation works." I took a step toward Handsome like it was my pet dog that was about to do tricks. I looked at it and said, "Hey Handsome, wave. Up."

The jumbled mess of a hand responded to my 'Up' command and started to move. It didn't have the support to actually do what it was supposed to do, so it just bounced around, looking somewhat like a wave.

There were a few laughs and claps from the audience. I looked at Sophie and my parents for reassurance. Somehow, it seemed to be going well, even though my project was a pile of robot poop. I know robots don't actually poop, not yet anyway, but you get my point.

"If we had more time and a gazillion dollars, we would expand on our idea in a few ways. For those potential users who are nonverbal, we could develop a headset to control Handsome, and perhaps a touchpad for those who have use of their hands but not legs. We could also add extensions to reach higher areas. Or perhaps even design entire storage systems that Handsome could use to deliver nearly everything a person could need in their home or office environment."

Ben nervously chimed in, "We could even program Handsome to pick noses and scratch butts. It's gross, but it's totally needed for people who can't do it themselves."

The crowd laughed.

"Thank you, Ben." I shook my head and continued, "Eventually, it will be cost effective for human parts to be replaced by robotic parts so that paralysis will be gone. You've probably seen robotic exoskeletons that help people walk, but they cost tens of thousands of dollars. In the meantime, a helping hand like Handsome here could be, well, very helpful."

I looked around, not knowing what else to say. "If you would like to meet Handsome, feel free to shake his hand. Just don't shake too hard. Thanks for listening."

The crowd erupted into cheers. I think it was mainly from my parents, Sophie, and Mr. Gifford, but I was happy anyway.

My parents rushed over to me, apparently believing that I needed to be embarrassed even more than I had already been. My mom hugged me. "Wonderful presentation," she said.

My dad joined the hug and squeezed. "You owned that. I'm so proud of you, bud."

"Thanks," I said, slowly squirming out of the hug.

I looked over to Ben. He was just getting the use of his appendages back. He wiggled his arms and then reached down to pick up his feet.

My parents finally let go after what seemed like an hour.

Mr. Muscalini stepped forward, "And that, Davenport, is the moment you became a man." He walked away without waiting for a response.

My parents looked at him like he was a lunatic. Which, of course, he was.

I said my goodbyes to my parents and I headed over to Max's to clean up.

I pushed open the door to Max's Comfort Station. He was waiting for me, as usual.

"Aus the Boss," he said, his voice trailing off. "What the heck happened to you?"

"Amanda Gluskin."

"Oooh. That's all I need to know." Max walked over to the cabinet. "I have just the thing."

"I knew this was the right place to come."

"Where else would you go? Did Donnie Felton open back up on the west wing?" Max asked, nervously.

"No. I would never go anywhere else," I said.

He placed a towel in my hand. "Oww," I said. I looked closer and noticed it was steaming.

"Just rub it on your face," Max said.

I did as I was told. The hot towel felt good on my face. When I was done, I handed it back to him. The glitter sparkled under the light of the chandelier. I looked up. Chandelier?

I looked toward the back of the bathroom. The hot tub was gone, replaced by an ornate mahogany dining table set for twelve.

"What the heck? Where did the hot tub go?"

"Energy costs were killing me, dude."

"So you bought a luxury dining set?"

"I hand carved it myself."

I stood there with my mouth open. "How did you get it in here?" I asked. None of it made any sense. I was waiting for him to tell me about his magical mirrors again, but he didn't.

He looked at me like I was an idiot and said, "The window." He nodded toward the line of back windows, none of them bigger than the ones in the locker room that I barely was able to climb through the night of the Halloween dance. Max Mulvihill was a true wizard. He bent the laws of physics somehow.

Max handed me a tube of something. I stopped staring at the windows and looked down at it. "What's this?"

"It's an exfoliating mud mask. We'll have your face shining like the morning sun in no time."

"Do you have anything that can give me a butt chin?" I asked, optimistic.

"Dude, I'm not Harry Potter."

I left Max and walked back to the gym, feeling better than I had in a long time. And my face felt spectacular, like a baby's butt. Except it didn't look like one. It was disappointing, but I'd lived without a butt chin my whole life. I could make it through another day.

As I headed down the main row, Sophie walked up to me, smiling. "Great job, Austin."

"Thanks. I'm just glad Ben didn't say anything embarrassing."

Sophie laughed. "Agreed. He kept it perfectly technical."

I laughed, too. I wanted to ask about what happened with Randy, but I was happy to just be happy with Sophie for what seemed like the first time in a long time. I had no glitter on my face and I was fully clothed. It was a pretty decent day.

After a long pause, Sophie said, "Randy denied cheating, but I know he did. I'm going to turn him in. It's the right thing to do."

I shook my head. "You can't prove that you weren't in on it. I don't trust him and Principal Buthaire at all- I would worry that you would get in just as much trouble, if not more. Don't do it. Just let it go."

"What if he wins? Or we win, I guess."

I shrugged. "Well, then let him win. We know he didn't. The last thing you want is Principal Buthaire on your bad side. At least that's what I hear."

Sophie laughed. "You're funny. When you're not throwing fish food in people's faces."

"That was an accident," I lied.

"You reached back and threw it as hard as you could!" Sophie said. She was more happy than mad.

"Okay, so I meant to do it. In hindsight, I'm pretty sure he deserved it."

Sophie didn't answer. She just smirked at me.

19

I t was award presentation time. I had no expectation of winning anything. I only hoped Randy would lose, so neither of us would win the bet. Plus, I still had to figure out how to unveil Randy's involvement in the website. I missed my chance with the news crew. I couldn't miss again with such a large crowd.

We all sat in the auditorium in our groups by the numbers we were given by Principal Buthaire, which meant I was five rows back from Sophie and Randy, who were in the front row.

Mr. Gifford stepped up to the podium and adjusted the microphone. "Welcome, Gophers!" he said, to a less-than-enthusiastic response.

Some kid yelled, "Nice beard!"

Mr. Gifford gave a thumbs up and continued, "This is the awards ceremony for the 44th annual Cherry Avenue Science Fair. We had a lot of great-" Mr. Gifford stopped as Principal Buthaire walked up onto the stage toward him. "Umm, we've had a lot of great entries and presentations-"

Principal Buthaire took the microphone from the stand on top of the podium. "Thank you, Mr. Gifford. Fabulous introduction as always."

There were two claps in the audience. Mr. Gifford slinked away.

Principal Buthaire walked out into the middle of the stage. "Welcome to the award presentation for the 44th Cherry Avenue science fair competition! It was a wonderful exhibition. I was interviewed for the news. It was a banner week for me-" He looked down at the crowd, talking amongst themselves.

"Err, what a banner week for the students of Cherry Avenue. Go Gophers!" Nobody clapped or cheered. He cleared his throat. "Moving on. Our first award goes to the best presentation as determined by our esteemed judges. Principal Buthaire walked over to the podium and picked up two cheap medals. He weighed them in his hand. "Wow, we went all out this year on the awards."

Some dude yelled out, "It looks like plastic!"

Principal Buthaire laughed nervously and ignored him. He held the microphone up and continued, "The students who won this award exemplify the Gopher spirit and are also a cute couple." He pulled an envelope out of his pocket and opened it. "Randy Warblemacher and Sophie Rodriguez! Come on up here!"

I missed a whole bunch of Butt Hair's speech because I was hurling on my shoes. I didn't care what I bet. I wasn't giving Randy my PlayStation, even though it really is Derek's.

Randy stood up to cheers, pumping his fist over his head. He looked at me and nodded his head like an arrogant dweeb. I watched Sophie as she stood up and followed

Randy to the stage. Randy headed up the stairs, but Sophie kept going.

Principal Buthaire said, "Uh, Ms. Rodriguez? Up here."

Sophie ignored him and continued walking below the stage toward the exit. The crowd was confused. Sophie walked to the doors and pushed them open. Randy stood on the stage next to Principal Buthaire, both of them not sure how to proceed.

Principal Buthaire put his arm around Randy and held the mic up to his face with the other. "Well, Sophie couldn't be with us this afternoon..."

I wanted to get up and follow her, but I was surrounded by at least ten kids on each side. Ugh. I decided to do it anyway. I stood up and scooted in front of Ben, my backpack over my shoulder.

Ben whispered, "Where are you going?"

"Sophie," I replied.

Principal Buthaire continued up on the stage. "Randy's cutting-edge project explored the transformative field of robotics. And he did so with excellence. And I am happy to report, I gave him the idea."

My ears nearly exploded. Gave him the idea? Was he serious? Did Prince Butt Hair steal the idea from me? He was outside my science class talking to Mrs. Lynch just before I told Mr. Gifford my project idea. He must have stolen it from me. I was so angry. I continued to half scoot, half climb over the rest of the kids in the row.

"And now we have the award for best presentation." Principal Buthaire began to open up the envelope. "This is very exciting. Our judges voted and-"

I thought that it was entirely possible that Randy and Sophie would sweep the science fair and win best project and best presentation, based on how well Sophie did. Randy even stood off to the side of the stage, seemingly having the same thought.

Principal Buthaire finished opening the envelope, pulled out the card, and read it. His face dropped. He whispered something away from the microphone. Nobody heard any of it.

"Who won?" Somebody called out from the crowd.

Principal Buthaire whispered, "Austin Davenport and Ben Gordon."

"Who? We can't hear you?"

"Austin Davenport and Ben Gordon," he said, louder. Prince Butt Hair looked like he was going to puke. He almost looked better than he usually did.

Cheers erupted from the crowd. I was engulfed by people patting me on my arms and backpack, and wishing me congratulations. I tried to continue making my way toward the door, following Sophie, but the crowd parted and pushed me toward the stage. I looked back at Ben and he was frozen in his seat.

Don't get me wrong, I was happy to win the award, but Sophie was more important to me than that. And I was less than enthused to join Prince Butt Hair up on the stage. I had no idea what embarrassing things he would say about me. I wondered if it was all a joke, just so he could give me a detention in front of everyone.

Randy and I passed each other on the stairs.

"Cheater," I whispered.

Randy didn't respond as he headed back to his seat.

I climbed up the stairs to the stage, watching Principal Buthaire's face with each step. He looked even less enthused than I did. The crowd was cheering as I made it up to the podium.

Someone yelled out, "Speech!"

Principal Buthaire, said, "Now, now. Calm down."

The crowd erupted into a chant, repeating, "Speech, speech, speech."

Principal Buthaire didn't know what to do. He held the microphone in his hand. I grabbed it from him. I had some things to say.

"I am grateful for the award. This is the first thing Principal Buthaire has given me that hasn't been detention." The crowd laughed. Principal Buthaire? Not so much.

I slipped off my backpack and looked at Principal Buthaire. "Actually," I continued, "I have something for you."

Principal Buthaire didn't look enthused. "What is it?"

I unzipped my backpack and pulled a Manila envelope from it. I handed the envelope to him. He stared at it, seemingly afraid to see what was inside.

"Don't worry, it's not going to bite." The crowd laughed again. "Since I was being blamed for the website about you, I uncovered the trail as to who owned the domain."

I looked down to the front of the crowd and caught Randy's eye. His face went white and his normally-cocky demeanor was nowhere to be found.

I continued, "It took me a while to figure it out, but here it is. Mystery solved." I handed Prince Butt Hair the microphone, put the medal around my neck, and starting walking off to cheers.

I grabbed Sophie's medal from the podium and said, "I'll give that to Sophie." I took her award and tucked it into my pocket.

Principal Buthaire didn't seem to care. He tore open the envelope like a savage and scanned all of the papers. He screamed into the mic, "Mr. Warblemacher! In my office immediately!"

The crowd ooohed and aahed. I smiled as I walked out of the room. Mic drop.

20

I rushed outside into the atrium. Dozens and dozens of kids and teachers roamed around. I searched for a few minutes and finally found Sophie sitting on a bench all alone. She looked up at me and smiled sheepishly.

I looked at the award in my hand, shrugged, and held it out for her.

"I don't want it," she said.

"It wasn't your fault. You still built a good project and made a nice presentation."

"The project wasn't real. It doesn't feel right winning like that," Sophie said.

She took the medal from me, stood up, and tossed it into the garbage pail at least five feet away.

I nodded, impressed. "Not bad. You ever think of trying out for the hoops team?"

"You sound like Mr. Muscalini," Sophie said, laughing.

"I can assure you that he's never said that to me."

We stared awkwardly at each other for a few seconds. I didn't know what else to say. "Umm, I guess I'll see you around."

Sophie smiled. "Guess so."

LATER THAT DAY, I sat in the kitchen, churning out an English paper on the pyramids in Mexico, which our family was set to visit in about six months. There was a knock at the door. I got up out of my chair and headed toward it. My mother beat me there. I stood behind her as she pulled open the door.

I peeked over her shoulder and saw a strange-looking robot, well, a person in a strange-looking robot costume. It looked like a silver droid from Star Wars.

My mother said, confused, "Umm, can I help you?"

"Hi, Mrs. Davenport. Is Austin here?"

My pulse started to race. The voice was a bit muffled, but it sounded like Sophie. What the heck was she doing here? And dressed like a robot?

"Yes. Who may I ask is, umm, asking?"

"Oh, sorry. It's Sophie, Mrs. Davenport."

"Oh, Sophie!" my mother said cheerfully. "Okay, sweetie. Hold on."

My mother stepped to the side, allowing me to step forward. I looked at her with a raised eyebrow. "Hey," I said. "Whatcha wearin'?"

"I was hoping that I was the droid you've been looking for."

She was going with the Star Wars theme. I decided to play along. "I thought so, but the droid I'm looking for knows how to dance."

"I guess I deserve that," Sophie said, of course, doing the robot dance. "Is that good?"

"A little more, just to be sure."

Sophie did some more roboting and even threw in a spin move.

"Nice," I said.

Sophie stopped and said, "So what do you say? Am I the droid you've been looking for?"

I may have been pressing my luck, but I said, "I felt like something was missing."

"In our relationship?" Sophie asked, confused.

"No. In your asking. I think you should use your robot voice."

"I don't...have a robot voice."

"Everybody has a robot voice. Try it out."

"You're so weird."

"Not helping."

"Sorry," Sophie said, and then in her best, but not great, robot voice, "Am...I...the...droid...you've...been...looking...for? Will...you...go...out...with...me?"

I robot walked toward her. "We...are...compatible." I tried to hug her, but it was on the awkward side. Which was par for the course, I guess.

"So, that's a yes?" Sophie asked, excited.

"I have some robot questions to ask you before I respond," I said, trying not to laugh.

"Austin, you never know when to quit."

I walked back in the house and pretended to shut the door.

"Okay..."

I opened the door back up and said, "Who is the best Transformer?"

"Umm, Optimus prime."

"Why did you hesitate?"

"I didn't," Sophie said, defensively.

"It's debatable. Hmm. What's the name of the lovable robot from the 1980s Classic, Short Circuit?"

"Ahhh, Johnny Five!"

"You are correct. Final question. What is my mother's favorite robot?"

"I don't know," Sophie said, shocked.

"Sorry. It's been nice knowing you."

"Wait! The Rumba!"

"That is correct!" I called out.

Derek chuckled behind me. "You and Ben are so weird."

I turned around. "That's not Ben! It's Sophie."

"OMG, you're such nerds," Derek said, hobbling away.

I shrugged. "Nerds unite!"

"More like nerds reunite," Sophie said.

I chuckled. We were interrupted by Derek yelling from the other room. "Oh, my God! Austin's on TV!"

I hid my face in my hands as we heard Calvin Conklin say full blast, "Next up on the six o'clock news: we interview the middle school girl who apprehended a boy time traveler. Man, did she kick his butt. It was mayhem." It sure was.

Sophie looked at me and laughed. "At least you have something to bond with Mr. Muscalini over."

I shrugged. It was true. I wasn't a time traveler, but we could bond over the butt kicking. Amanda Gluskin had Camel Clutched us both. Believe me, if I was a time traveler, I'd make sure that none of this story ever happened.

21

BOOK 4 PREVIEW CHAPTER

MIDDLE SCHOOL MAYHEM: BATTLE OF THE BANDS

I'm going to let you in on a little secret. Nerds have one chance, just one, to be cool in middle school and high school. If you can't catch a football or don't look like a movie star with a butt chin like my brother, here is my advice to you: start a band. It doesn't even have to be that good of a band. You just have to be able to say that you're in one and it has to have a good name. Something cool. Something that gives you street cred. I don't know where some of these famous bands today get their names. I mean, Twenty One Pilots? Are there really twenty one pilots in the band and if so, why? What are they actually all doing? And what about Weezer? Do they all have asthma? Sounds like half the kids in my robotics club, not a band.

I had never even thought about being in a band for the first ten years of my life. I didn't even know I liked singing or was even good at it until my first year in middle school when I tried out for the holiday musical, Santukkah! But that's a story for another time. You may have even heard it already. But back to the band. It all started after I had made it through sixth grade at Cherry Avenue Middle School and we were off for a glorious summer vacation. As far as I was concerned, there were two good things about middle school: weekends and summer vacations. I was pumped to have ten weeks of summer ahead of me.

I mainly spent my summers at Camp Cherriwacka, a day camp near my house that I liked for the most part. But camp wasn't a total escape from the chaos that was middle school. A lot of the kids from Cherry Avenue went to camp with us. So did other middle schoolers from other districts. So, the usual rules and social hierarchy still applied, but everyone was a little more laid back and spread out.

The bus pulled up to Camp Cherriwacka's entrance and screeched to a stop. Ben and I hopped out first with our friends, Sammie, Luke Hill, and Just Charles behind us. My brother (the one with the giant butt chin and so very annoying) and his friend, Jayden, sat in the back with the cool kids. We were in the same grade, but he was almost a year older than me and a lot better at most stuff than I was. That's not why I didn't like him or his butt chin, but I won't get into that now.

As we walked through the wooded pathway heading toward the common area, there was a boy sitting under a tree just off the path. He paid us no attention as he played an acoustic guitar, singing to himself. He had dirty blonde hair that waved down to his shoulders.

"Man, I wish I was that cool and could do that," I said.

"Who is that guy?" Ben asked.

"I don't know. This camp pulls in from a few different schools. He wasn't here last year."

"I thought your dad taught you how to play the guitar a few years ago?" Sammie asked. We had been friends since she moved next door to me when we were three.

"He did, but I never got that good and it's been a while

since I've even picked one up," I said as we continued walking.

A man in cargo shorts, a Hawaiian shirt, and an oversized safari hat stood next to the pool entrance with a smile on his face even bigger than his hat. "Good morning!" he bellowed. Well, as much as you can bellow with a high-pitched nasally voice. "You can put your bags near the cabana and gather 'round the pool."

We walked into the pool area. My sister, Leighton, was setting up a breakfast buffet on the other side of the pool. She looked over and waved to me. I waved back as I threw my stuff on the ground. It was Leighton's first year as a camp counselor at Camp Cherriwacka. There were a few other counselors around as well. Some I knew from previous years. Others were new like Leighton.

I felt a tap on my shoulder. I turned around. It was Sophie, my girlfriend. I was so happy to see her. I greeted her with my customary, "Hey!"

"Hey," she said back. Our relationship was so deep, we didn't really need to say much to each other. Or at least that's what I kept telling myself.

"I'm so glad Sammie talked you into coming to camp," I said.

"Me, too. I heard it's really fun."

As the kids gathered around the pool, the man from the entrance stepped forward, still with the same smile as before. I wondered if it somehow was stuck on his face. He just watched everyone as they went about their business. Nobody was that smiley all the time. I looked around at the other kids. I saw a few kids I knew from last year, a few others from school, and the guitar kid from before.

If I had a smile on my face at that time, it was most definitely gone by the time I finished scanning the group of kids. My stomach dropped as my arch nemesis, Randy Warblemacher, entered in slow motion.

Randy was a cool kid, at least that's what most of the idiots at school thought. I was not at all a fan. He was a liar, a cheater, and a bully. But man, did he have glorious hair and a fabulous singing voice. He handed his bag to the smiling man and shook out his hair like he was in a shampoo commercial. His golden lochs bounced around like homecoming cheerleaders. Sammie and a few of the other girls giggled. Ditzy Dayna nearly fell over. Randy grabbed his bag back and dropped it off next to the rest of them.

The smiling man stepped forward and said, "Good morning, campers! My name is Kevin Quackenbush. I am the new camp director. We're going to have a fabulous summer. Who's ready to have some fun?" he yelled.

We were middle schoolers, so instead of answering, we all just looked around to see who would be stupid enough to say anything. You make that mistake once. Mine was when the science fair was announced. I make no apologies. I like science.

Kevin's smile persisted. "Looks like we have a very animated group this year! You're going to meet your counselors real quick, then grab a bite to eat at the breakfast buffet, and then we have a special treat to start the summer off right. Who's with me?" he screamed, excitedly.

Silence. "Excellent! You all have your group numbers. We'll line the counselors up in order. Go get to it, campers!"

I turned to Sophie and said, "See you later." I watched her as she walked toward Leighton with Sammie. My sister was going to be my girlfriend's camp counselor. Leighton and I got along better than Derek and I did, but I still wasn't sure this whole thing was a good idea. I was just glad Derek and Randy were in a different group.

I stopped in front of camp counselor number four, Brody Foster. Ben, Luke, Just Charles, the guitar kid, and a few others all stood in silence.

Brody stood a foot taller than most of us. I guessed that he was a few years into high school. He brushed the hair out of his eyes and stepped forward. I was excited to hear about all the cool things we would be doing this summer. Camp Cherriwacka always had awesome new stuff to do.

Brody cleared his throat and said, "This is going to be a great summer experience for you. Just pretend I'm not here. I mean, I'll make sure none of you die or anything like that, if I can, but I'll mainly be on my phone or trying to get that cute new counselor to go out with me."

Ben nudged me and said, "Dude, I think he's talking about your sister."

Brody continued, "So, we're the dork group. They put all the jocks together in one group and you guys together. You know, it's like the zoo. They don't want to mix predator and prey. Death is bad for business." He shrugged. "I guess that's it. Enjoy the breakfast and the music. We'll meet back here after. Maybe." Brody walked away.

I looked at my friends. "Geez, that's harsh."

The guitar kid stepped toward us, shaking his head. "Dorks? You think I would be in the dorks' group? We're the lovers, not the fighters."

Another boy followed. He had dark hair that was a tad too long for his glasses, and arms and legs that were too long for the rest of him. He was like a four-limbed spider.

"Yeah, we're lovers." Just Charles said, not entirely confident about it.

I put out my hand to shake the new kid's hand. "I'm Austin. This is Ben, Just Charles, and Luke."

He shook my hand. "You got a girl, Aus?"

"Yep. Sophie. She's here at camp. How 'bout you?"

"Nah, man. Not lookin' to settle down in the summer time, you know what I mean?"

I just nodded, but I had no idea what he was talking about. I was just thankful that any girl liked me, especially Sophie. You don't break up with a girl like Sophie because it's summer time. Amanda Gluskin? Maybe. If you were dumb enough to date her in the first place.

"Why aren't you with the cool kids?" Ben asked.

"Here's a secret for you. You can be cool without being an athlete," the still unnamed guitar kid said.

"You can?" Luke asked.

"Absolutely. I'm Sly, by the way. This is Teddy."

"That's a cool name," I said. "What's your last name?"

"Don't need one," Sly said, simply.

"Why not?" Just Charles asked.

"Because my name is Sly. That's all you need to know. How many other kids are named Sly that you know?"

"None," Just Charles said, shrugging.

"So why do I need a last name?" Sly looked over at the breakfast buffet. "Breakfast is served. Catch you guys later, yo." Sly walked over toward the buffet with Teddy on his heels.

"He never told us the secret," Just Charles whispered, disappointed.

"Man, that dude is cool," I said.

"Yeah. People with one name are so cool," Ben said.

Luke added. "And he plays the guitar."

I walked back over to the buffet and grabbed a plate next to Sophie. She smiled at me and said, "I love your sister," Sophie said, enthusiastically. "She's awesome. How's your counselor?"

"Umm, not as good as yours."

"Awww, that's so sweet. I didn't know you felt that way about your sister," Sophie said, smiling.

It wasn't what I meant. I wasn't giving my sister a compliment. It was more about Brody stinking up the place, but I wasn't going to correct her. She called me sweet.

And then seemingly out of nowhere, Kevin Quackenbush called out, "I give you Goat Turd!"

Most of the campers cheered. Goat turd? Why the heck did the camp director want to give us goat poop? I looked over at Kevin and he was pointing at a rock band of five musicians that promptly started playing.

Most of the girls in camp rushed toward the mini stage and started shrieking like wackos.

"Oh, my God! That's Cameron Quinn!" Sammie said, nearly knocking me over. "He's so cool!"

"Who the heck is that?" I asked.

"He's the lead singer of Goat Turd," Sophie said, like I was supposed to know that.

I was a little jealous, but Sophie wasn't nearly as crazy as the rest of them, so I just tried to focus on the performance. The girls hung on every word he sang. I must admit, he was pretty awesome. He sang like a pro as he danced across the stage. Just being able to do one of them was impressive, but together, he was a star. Even a bunch of the dudes crowded around the stage and started jumping up and down as Goat Turd rocked out.

Cameron Quinn stood next to the electric guitarist in the group near the center of the small stage. He put the mic to his mouth and yelled, "Are you ready?"

I wasn't sure what he was talking about, but the crowd seemed to. They all screamed. Cameron ran straight toward the edge of the stage and jumped off it. He soared through the air and twisted, landing on his back in the outstretched hands of the mini-mob in front of him. The kids in the crowd held Cameron over their heads, passing him through the crowd.

A girl yelled, "Oh, my God! I touched him!"

When Cameron made it to the end of the crowd, he fell gracefully to his feet, landing next to a girl by the breakfast buffet. She stared into his eyes, mesmerized, holding a piece of toast inches from her open mouth. With the microphone in one hand, Cameron grabbed the girl's toast and took a bite. He handed it back to her, turned, and ran up the few steps back onto the stage.

The toast girl yelled, "O.M.G. We shared breakfast!" She looked at the girl next to her and asked, "That's like a date, right?"

"Totally...He might've even tasted your spit, so you kinda made out with him!"

Toast Girl was giddy. I just stood there staring as Goat Turd rocked the stage. I had never seen a live show of any band that good. I wasn't going to scream like a crazy wacko, but I was in awe.

AFTER THE GOAT TURD PERFORMANCE, Sophie, Sammie, and I stood facing Ben and Just Charles, the pool behind them, munching on bagels and muffins.

Sly walked over. "What's up, guys? And girls?"

Luke looked over at a crowd of girls. "Who is that with Annie Hesselbeck?"

We all looked over. I remembered Annie Hesselbeck from last year. All I really knew about her was that she was tall and always wore her strawberry hair in a ponytail. And always too tight so that she seemed confused or perhaps squinting to see what was going on in the distance. There was a girl next to her who looked like a model. The giant fan blew her blond hair back like she was on a photo shoot.

"That's Regan Storm. She's from Bear Creek. She's unlikable," Sophie said, distastefully.

"I don't think her parents even like her," Sammie said. She looked at me. "I think your sister is going to get fired for punching her in the face before the end of the summer."

Luke apparently didn't hear any of that, still mesmerized by Regan Storm. "We're lovers, right?" he said to Ben, Just Charles, and Sly.

"Yep," Sly said. "You learn fast."

"What are you talking about?" Ben asked. Apparently, Ben didn't learn as fast.

Luke said, "You heard what Sly said, 'We're lovers, not fighters.' Let's show those jocks that they've got some competition." Luke nodded in the direction of Derek, Randy, and Jayden.

"Here they come," Just Charles said, nervously.

I looked over at Ben and I could see his body start to stiffen. His muscles always froze when he got nervous. It typically ends in disaster. Hopeful that this time will be different? You shouldn't be. Like, at all.

"What's up?" Luke said to the approaching girls.

"Hi," Regan said with a smile. Annie followed her quietly. And seemingly confused.

None of the 'lovers' in the group knew what to say. Regan walked in between the two sides of our group and stood in front of Ben. "What's up with this one? He's kinda cute."

Ben just stared at her. He usually only maintained control of his ears and his mouth. Unfortunately, he usually was able to speak, but with about half his normal brain power. This time, I wasn't sure if he still had control of his ears.

"The shy type. I like that," Regan said, stepping closer toward him. "Have you ever kissed a girl?"

We all just watched like it was the bottom of the ninth in game seven of the World Series. The home team was down by three with the bases loaded and the injured superstar was called upon to win the game with a grand slam. I know I'm a nerd, but my brother plays baseball. Anyway, none of us knew what to do. Luke's mouth was wide open. Just Charles was so nervous about Ben, he was sweating. Was she going to kiss him? Was he going to make a fool of himself? The answer is yes to one of those questions.

And then Ben spoke. "Well, my mom. And grandma. She kind of has a mustache so I have to say I don't enjoy those kisses."

I had a really bad feeling about it all, but I didn't know what to do.

Regan stepped closer to him. "Do you want to kiss me?"

"In front of everyone?" Ben asked. He looked at me. I shrugged. I know, I was a great help.

"This is going to be an amazing summer," Regan said, putting both hands on his shoulders.

"Okay." Ben puckered his lips.

Regan said, "Hashtag, are you serious, nerd?" She threw her head back and cackled. She pushed Ben with both hands and laughed as Ben teetered over like a giant statue, and fell into the pool, fully clothed, in front of the whole camp.

ABOUT THE AUTHOR

C.T. Walsh is the author of the Middle School Mayhem Series, set to be a total twelve hilarious adventures of Austin Davenport and his friends.

Besides writing fun, snarky humor and the occasionally-frequent fart joke, C.T. loves spending time with his family, coaching his kids' various sports, and successfully turning seemingly unsandwichable things into spectacular sandwiches, while also claiming that he never eats carbs. He assures you, it's not easy to do. C.T. knows what you're thinking: this guy sounds complex, a little bit mysterious, and maybe even dashingly handsome, if you haven't been to the optometrist in a while. And you might be right.

C.T. finds it weird to write about himself in the third person, so he is going to stop doing that now.

You can learn more about C.T. (oops) at ctwalsh.fun

facebook.com/ctwalshauthor

goodreads.com/ctwalsh

ALSO BY C.T. WALSH

Down with the Dance: Book One

Santukkah!: Book Two

Battle of the Bands: Book Four

Made in the USA
Columbia, SC
16 November 2020